About Apollo Africa

The original Heinemann African Writers Series was launched in 1962 with the publication of Chinua Achebe's *Things Fall Apart*, Cyprian Ekwensi's *Burning Grass* and Kenneth Kaunda's *Zambia Shall Be Free*, with Achebe himself acting as an editorial advisor. Over the next 40 years, the series continued to publish the best writing from across the African continent.

One of the founding aims of the Heinemann series was to make books by African writers available to as wide a readership as possible. Apollo Africa – a collaboration between Black Star Books and Head of Zeus – is proud to continue this work, ensuring novels, essays, poetry and plays from the original series are once again made available to readers all over the world.

Hill of Fools

Hill of Fools

R.L. Peteni

Black Star Books and Head of Zeus would like to thank the following organisations: The Miles Morland Foundation, The Ford Foundation, and Africa No Filter. This publication was made possible through their support.

First published in the Heinemann African Writers Series in 1976 by Heinemann Educational Publishers

This edition published in 2024 by Black Star Books and Head of Zeus, part of Bloomsbury Publishing Plc.

Copyright © R.L. Peteni, 1976

The moral right of R.L. Peteni to be identified as the author of this work has been asserted in accordance with the Copyright, Designs and Patents Act of 1988.

All rights reserved. No part of this publication may be reproduced, stored in a retrieval system, or transmitted in any form or by any means, electronic, mechanical, photocopying, recording, or otherwise, without the prior permission of both the copyright owner and the above publisher of this book.

This reprint is published by arrangement with Pearson Education Limited.

This is a work of fiction. All characters, organizations, and events portrayed in this novel are either products of the author's imagination or are used fictitiously.

9 7 5 3 1 2 4 6 8

A catalogue record for this book is available from the British Library.

ISBN (PB): 9781035900824
ISBN (E): 9781803288468

Typeset by Siliconchips Services Ltd UK

Printed and bound in Great Britain by
CPI Group (UK) Ltd, Croydon CR0 4YY

Head of Zeus Ltd
First Floor East
5–8 Hardwick Street
London EC1R 4RG

WWW.HEADOFZEUS.COM

Chief Characters

(Clan names are in brackets)

In Kwazidenge, the Hlubi village
Mvangeli Langa (Bhele)
Mrs Mamiya Langa
Duma, one of their sons
Zuziwe, their daughter

Vukubi Langa, Mvangeli's brother
Katana, his son

Khubalo (Bhele)

Dakada (Ndlovu)
Mrs Mamtolo Dakada
Ntombi, their daughter
Zisani, their son

Ntabeni Mlilo (Thole), the Ndlovus' nephew
Zanele, his sister
Makhwenkwe, his nephew

Mlenzana Nqaba

Diliza Mququ

Makaziwe Godlwana: girl of the village
Nomi Nqwelo: girl of the village
Nompongo Sophunga: girl of the village

Mulungisi Nkabi

Ngalweni Nkonde: warrior boy of the village
Matshanda: warrior boy of the village
Khanda: warrior boy of the village

In the Thembu village
Bhuqa Ngoma
Notizi, his sister

Zuziwe's uncle (Nkala) and aunt

Tozi: girl of the village
Nozikade: girl of the village

Gabulamehlo, sanuse
Mathambo, his assistant

Dr Sango, medical doctor

In these communities, first cousins would often be called brother and sister, and paternal uncles and aunts called mother and father.

Glossary

Xhosa Word	*English Equivalent*
Amasi	Sour milk
Bafondini	Men (vocative case)
Bawo	Father
Bawokazi	Father's younger brother
Bhoma	Initiates' grass hut
Bhuti/Bhut'	Elder brother
Ewe	Yes
Hayi	No
Isinga	Cluster of mimosa trees
Khankatha	Guardian-instructor
Kwedini	Boy (vocative case)
Lobola	Dowry (paid by the young man)
MaBhele	People of the Bhele clan
Madoda	Men
Makwedini	Boys (vocative case)
Malume	Maternal uncle
Mama	Mother
Mbhayizelo	Form of dance with grunting noise
Mfazi	Woman
Mhlekazi	Your worship
Mkhuluwa	Elder brother
Molo	Greetings (to one person)

Molweni	Greetings (to many people)
Mnquma	Olive tree
Msenge	Cabbage-wood tree
Msimbithi	Cape ebony wood
Mthathi	Sneezewood tree
Mvangeli	Evangelist
Mvubo	Mixture of ground boiled corn and amasi
Myeke	Let him be
Mzala	Cousin
Ndiyeke	Unhand me
Nkosikazi	Woman or wife
Ntanga	An equal in age
Ntombi yam	My daughter/my girl
Nyana	Son
Sana	Baby
Sanuse	Witchdoctor/diviner
Satanandini	You Satan
Sies (Afrikaans)	Expression of disgust
Sinquma	Cluster of olive trees
Siphingo	Thorn bush with edible black berries
Sisi/Sis'	Elder sister
Sithandwa	Loved one
Tata	Father
Thula	Be quiet
Tolofiya	Prickly-pear
Udlalani	Playboy

Place Names

Bhukazana	Hogsback
Mthwaku	St Matthews
Nkonkobe	Winterberg
Qoboqobo	Keiskamahoek
Qonce	King William's Town
Xesi	Keiskama (river)

1 | *The Village Beauty*

Mvangeli Langa's youngest child, Zuziwe, was a very beautiful girl. She was the undeclared beauty queen of the Hlubi village of Kwazidenge, which lay snugly at the foot of the Hill of Fools, five miles south-west of Qoboqobo town in the Eastern Cape. She was the only daughter in a family of five children; and, being the child of Mr and Mrs Langa's old age, she was rather spoilt. Her parents had grown into the habit of protecting her from her rough brothers; and they continued to protect her even when she was no longer a child. Zuziwe enjoyed her privileged position. Some of her elder brothers had married when she was still too young to do housework, and had brought their wives to live with them at their parents' home, for this was the way of all families living at Kwazidenge village. The young wives had fallen into the habit of doing all the housework, leaving nothing for their young sister-in-law to do. Zuziwe on her part was fond of washing and preening herself and admiring her lovely face and shapely curves in the large bedroom mirror.

The only task Zuziwe chose for herself was the afternoon walk to the spring nearby, or to the river a mile away, to fetch water for household use. She liked this task because there was an element of adventure in it, and she loved excitement and adventure with all her heart. Once, when she was still a very young girl, a mere child, her brothers had dared her to go to the spring alone to fetch water in her little tin. They had told her of slimy snakes and wild beasts and ugly dwarfs which she would meet on the way. The little girl had accepted the challenge. She had gone alone to the spring, although with set face and bulging eyes. She had returned with only half a tin of water. The other half had spilt over and soaked her frock because she could not balance the tin properly on her head. She had looked to the left and the right and the back, for fear of snakes and beasts and dwarfs.

Zuziwe had now outgrown her fear of dwarfs and other horrors, but not her love of adventure. She was still queen of the Langa home and was more beautiful than any other girl in Kwazidenge. Her beauty made her unpopular with other girls of her age. The older men of the village were outspoken in praise of her beauty, and the younger men could not hide their interest in her. This made the other girls hate her. They agreed among themselves that she was a loose girl, that she deliberately tried to steal their lovers and that a slight push from a man was enough to make her lie on her back. Zuziwe grew increasingly lonely and friendless as she grew older. She went quite often to the river to fetch water, sometimes in the company of her brothers' wives, sometimes alone. There were no snakes, no beasts, no dwarfs to fear; but there were often mischievous boys to lend excitement and adventure to the walk. Her parents often warned her against walking alone to the river. They told her that some boys were bad and that they would assault her one day. Zuziwe remembered that her brothers had tried to frighten her when she was younger, and that she had refused to be frightened. She had proved to herself and to them that she was not a coward. So, she did not listen to her parents' warning. On the contrary, it stirred up the spirit of adventure in her. She was determined to show that she, who feared neither snake nor beast nor dwarf, was not afraid of a mere boy.

Zuziwe left her home later than usual one day to go to the river. As she was walking slowly down the footpath, she was joined by Diliza of tolofiya section of Kwazidenge.

'Molo, Zuziwe. May I accompany you?'

'Molo, Diliza. You may if you like. But I'm not afraid. I need no escort.' The girl spoke in a voice as sweet as a bird's voice, and with a smile so bright that it brought a rush of blood to the young man's head.

'You do need an escort, Zuziwe. The river is not safe. Thembu boys sometimes cross over to our side.'

'What is it to me if they cross over? There's nothing they can rob me of. They wouldn't take my bucket from me. Empty or full, they have no use for it.'

'You're talking nonsense, Zuziwe. You know very well that a Thembu boy has no right to set foot on Hlubi soil.'

'Why?' asked Zuziwe.

'What do you mean "why"? He has no right to do so, that's all. And you ought to know that and teach it to your children as it must have been taught to you, though you seem to have forgotten it.'

'I'd rather have no children than teach them such nonsense. I have relatives and friends living in the Thembu village. My malume, my own mother's brother, lives there. My malume's children are among those you describe as bad boys. Yet I know they are good boys, as good as any you will find in the Hlubi village. They always treat me like a sister when I visit them. Some of the Thembu girls are my friends and they have brothers who are friendly to me. Why should I hate people who have never hurt me? Why should you, Diliza, hate and wish to hurt people who have never hurt you?'

'I hate them because I must. I was brought up to hate them. I know that a Thembu boy must be attacked and hit very hard and be killed. Don't ask me why I must kill them. Ask the sun and the moon and the stars. Ask the rain and the wind. Ask the mountains, the valleys and the rivers; the trees, the grass and the flowers. Ask the insects and the beasts and the birds. Don't ask me. Ask the maker of these things and the maker of me. If you ask me why I must kill the Thembus, you may as well ask the wind why it blows dust into my eyes, or the sun why it dries up the streams, or the bee why it stings me and the snake why it bites me. I can no more suppress my urge to kill than the other creatures which God created. If I didn't believe that a Thembu boy must be destroyed, I would not be a true Hlubi boy. There would be something wrong with me, as there must be something wrong with a Hlubi girl who does not feel as we boys feel in this matter. Or are you saying all this because you have smiled on one of these Thembu boys?'

Zuziwe did not answer. She was disgusted with Diliza for his mad love of violence. She walked on, hoping that he would go back to the Hill of Fools with his madness and that she could walk to the river alone, there to have her pleasant thoughts and her quietness and peace of mind restored to her by the soothing voice of the river and its cool healing waters. But Diliza did not leave her in peace. He walked up to her. Zuziwe stopped and looked at him with fear in her eyes, for she knew he was a wild bull, a coarse, rough beast, rough even on girls. He took her hand and held it firmly and looked her in the eyes.

'Are you in love with a Thembu boy, Zuziwe?' he asked.

'*Thix' onofefe!* Merciful God! Are you my husband or my lover that you ask me such a question? I know you have often asked for my love, but I don't remember giving it to you. What right have you, then, to ask me about my love affairs, and what business of yours is it anyway?'

'Don't speak to me like that, you rubbish, or I'll hit you on that filthy mouth of yours.'

'You've been praised too much for your bravery. It has spoilt you, I see. Now you want to hit a girl. That's no bravery. That's cowardice, let me tell you. Go on then. Hit me so that you may go about boasting about it. But you'll regret it. I have brothers who are not afraid of you.'

'Brothers! Nonsense! I can make any of your brothers eat mud. I'm not afraid of them. But I'll spare you because of Katana, though I'm sorry that my best friend should have such a slut for a sister.'

Diliza released Zuziwe's hand and pushed her so violently that she nearly fell. He shut his ears to her angry words and went back to the village. Zuziwe sat on a stone on one side of the narrow, winding path and burst into tears of anger. Then she remembered that her tears would not improve her appearance. She forced them back and dried her eyes with the towelling cloth wrapped round her head. Diliza was not the only boy in the village. She was likely to meet others not so rude. Her looks, after all, were very important to her. It was well known that boys were wild in their ways. So why should she be upset by the rudeness of the wildest of these boys?

The Xesi river is not an important river as far as rivers go. But to the villagers of Kwazidenge it is as important as the Nile to Egyptians, the Thames to Englishmen, the Vaal to South Africans. It rises in the Mathole mountains, twists and turns round mountains and hills, cuts through the coastal belt, and joins the Indian Ocean a few miles west of East London. It never runs dry, even in winter when rains are scarce. One of its most important tributaries is the Zingcuka river, which is fed by numerous, silver-white mountain streams. But the main source of the Zingcuka is a lake of crystal-clear water on the summit of the Bhukazana mountain. This lake is fed by water from the interior of the earth and, according to legend, is the home of a mysterious water snake which feeds on dirty objects in the lake and helps to keep the water clean. For this reason the waters of the Zingcuka river are always clear, even in summer when it overflows its banks.

But not the waters of the Xesi river. When the heavy rains come, the Xesi river becomes an agent of death, with its waters the colour of blood, the blood of overpopulated, impoverished, dismal villages. The life-giving soil is washed from the grain lands by rushing torrents which follow in the wake of severe droughts and furious hailstorms, giving the river the dark colour of blood. The river swells into a raging torrent and becomes a monster which destroys people, animals and crops along the river valley. But the normal function of the river is to give life to both the Thembu village and the Hlubi village impartially. The frowning, unscaleable cliffs on its banks are shared by both sides equally, or almost equally. On the Hlubi side there are tall trees under which herds of cattle lie after they have drunk their fill of water in the river. Lower down, on the Thembu side, the river spreads out into a natural swimming pool, with a shallow end for younger children and a deep end with a large flat stone at the water's edge, from which good swimmers jump into the water. A short distance away from this natural swimming pool there is a stretch of open ground that is always covered with green grass. This spot is the favourite meeting-place of the girls and boys of the Thembu village. Here they hold the Sunday afternoon song and dance meeting known as mbhayizelo. Here they play their favourite sport, the stick-fight, on Christmas day or New Year's Day or a wedding day. Here they meet to arrange their seasonal entertainment programmes.

The ford which enables the Thembus and the Hlubis to cross the river is at this spot, just above the swimming pool. Long ago, some enterprising, public-spirited villagers brought large stones which they arranged as stepping stones for crossing the river and facilitating communication between the two villages. They set the stones firmly in the bed of the river, and here they remain, year after year, ensuring the safety of all who cross the river. But not even the oldest of the villagers is old enough to know who rendered this service to the two communities.

The young women and the girls come to the ford to

fetch water for use in their homes, except during the rainy season when the rainwater from the roofs of the houses fills the water tanks, and the fountains near the village are full of clear, cool, delicious water from the interior of the earth. These young women love to come in groups, in the cooler hours of the late afternoon. They recount their experiences or exchange gossip on the events of the day, on the stupidity of husbands and the tyranny of fathers, on the infidelity of boyfriends and the looseness of rival beauties, on the ungodliness of churchmen and the greed of wealthy villagers, on the naughtiness of neighbours' children and the cleverness of their own, on the ravages of disease and the evil hearts of sorcerers. They cruise along from topic to topic without introduction and without conclusion. Their conversation is often punctuated by loud, uninhibited laughter or exclamation, a welcome relief after the suppression to which most of the young wives are subjected in their marital homes.

They take their time. The wives are in no hurry to return home. As for the girls, there is a better chance of being seen and spoken to by young men if they take a long time at the river. So, they relax. They wash their hands, their arms, their faces, their feet, their legs, and even their thighs. Some wash their armpits and their breasts. They have grown skilled at the art of washing almost the entire body in this manner, in instalments. Then they rub themselves with oil or fat, which is believed to have the power of opening the eyes of young men to the beauty of their bodies. They rub their faces and their legs, the conspicuous parts of the body, until they shine in the afternoon sun and send bright reflections from the clear waters of the Xesi river.

And so Zuziwe went slowly down to the popular ford after her encounter with Diliza. She found many Thembu children swimming in the river. They were young boys and girls, all much younger than she was. So, she did not join in the fun, although she yearned for the cool water, and for the complete self-abandon which she used to enjoy in the river pool when she was of an age and size to undress herself and plunge naked into the water. It could be great fun, she knew, to swim and splash in the water, or dive in the deeper parts if you had the skill. The fun had its layer of harmless mischief, as when a naughty boy dived into the water with her and snatched a quick kiss and tickled her breasts. She pushed him off after allowing him to tickle her for a second, enjoying the sensation. It could be so delightful to be embraced in the water, the slippery, naked bodies touching each other, charged with electrical, youthful vitality. Afterwards, when the boy tried to catch her eye, she knitted her eyebrows and frowned and looked beyond him, to make him understand that the incident under the water meant nothing at all. Zuziwe envied the children playing and swimming in the water. She wondered why one must give up the pleasures of childhood even if one still longed for them. Why must one give up these childhood delights when there were no substitutes for them for girls of her age?

'Molo, Zuziwe,' said a voice close behind her.

Zuziwe turned round with a suppressed scream. She was so startled that she nearly fell off the large stone on which she was seated at the water's edge.

'Oh, Bhuqa, what a fright you gave me. When did you come? I didn't see you. I didn't even hear you come,'

'Molo, Zuziwe,' said Bhuqa again. 'You haven't responded to my greeting.'

'Oh, molo, Bhuqa. Please excuse me. You really startled me with that deep voice of yours.'

'I've been watching you from that small island in the middle of the river. I stood behind those trees for some time. Are you longing to join the children in the water? I noted the look in your eyes. I saw you smile once. When I looked at the children, I saw nothing particularly amusing. You must have been smiling at something in your mind. What was it, Zuziwe?'

'It was some pleasant childhood memory which I will not tell to you.'

'Is it a secret, then? Is it something bad?'

'I don't care what questions you ask me; I won't tell it to you. What have you to do with a girl's secrets? Please, let's talk of something else.'

Bhuqa smiled and sat beside Zuziwe on the stone, his legs dangling and reaching into the water. He was a bright-eyed, intelligent-looking lad of the 'big boy' class, the warrior class. His complexion was neither dark nor light but more the colour of copper. He was of medium height and build and looked tough and sinewy. He had a pleasant face, which could change and look ugly and dangerous when he frowned. But when he was smiling and at ease, he was handsome. He was popular with other boys because he was a pleasant companion.

Zuziwe's wistful look had touched Bhuqa. He knew her fairly well. She and his younger sister, Notizi, were close friends. They were often together when Zuziwe visited her uncle and aunt in the Thembu village, which she did quite frequently despite the hostility between the two villages. But Bhuqa had always taken her for a little girl. Zuziwe was two years younger than he was. Today, however, he had suddenly realized that she was a full-grown girl, beautiful, attractive, desirable. But how was he to talk to her on matters of love when he had always regarded her and treated her as a child? So, he remained quiet and thoughtful for a long time until Zuziwe spoke.

'I must leave you alone with your thoughts, Bhuqa,' she said. 'I must go and wash myself and fill my bucket with water and go home.'

'No, wait a little, Zuziwe,' he said quickly. 'I've something to ask you.'

'Ask me then, and be quick about it,' replied Zuziwe cheerfully. 'It's getting late.'

'What do you mean "it's getting late"?' asked Bhuqa. 'You were sitting there, quite comfortable, when I came. What has suddenly made it late?'

'I was about to go. I've stayed here too long. My parents always get worried and anxious if I return home late. They say there are bad boys at this river.'

'What do you say?' asked Bhuqa in a challenging tone. 'If there are bad boys at all, they must be on your side. Our boys are well behaved. They never interfere with Hlubi girls.'

'But what is it you want to ask?'

'When will you visit your uncle at our village? It's a long time since you were there, if I remember well. I'm sure your uncle's family and your friend, Notizi, all miss you.'

'You had better mind your own business, big boy,' replied Zuziwe, smiling. 'It's no business of yours whether they miss me or not.'

'It is my business, Zuziwe,' replied Bhuqa softly, and then, after a short pause, he looked Zuziwe straight in the eyes and added, 'I miss you too.'

'How can you miss me when I'm here next to you?'

'I do miss you. I should like you to visit our village because I hope to see you then and ask you something for which there's no time now.'

'What is this which requires a longer time than the time we've been together now? Is it some long story you want to tell me, or a sermon you wish to preach? You will certainly not be with me for a long time when I visit my uncle.'

'When will that be?'

'Perhaps next week, or next month, or next year. Only God in heaven knows. So you had better speak now if what you wish to ask is so important.'

'It is important, and it cannot wait indefinitely. I love you, Zuziwe.'

'That's not a question, Bhuqa, that's a statement. You said you had a question to ask.'

'I'll make it a question, if you like. Do you love me, Zuziwe?'

'If I like? Are you asking that question because I like? Who told you that that is what I like?'

'Don't twist my words, Zuziwe, sithandwa. Say you love me.'

Zuziwe was indeed teasing Bhuqa. She had known within the first few minutes of his arrival that he had fallen in love with her. She on her part had always been attracted by him and by his obvious interest in her. But she was engaged to be married to Ntabeni Mlilo, who was a well-to-do Hlubi villager. It was the wish of Zuziwe's family, especially her brothers, that she should marry Ntabeni. Poor Zuziwe was confused. Deep down in her heart she felt more attracted to Bhuqa than Ntabeni, but she felt compelled by her respect for her family and her fear of her brothers to continue her relationship with Ntabeni. So she decided to move slowly, hoping that time would clear things up and help her make a good decision.

'No, Bhuqa,' she replied after a long time, 'I cannot say I love you.'

'Why not? Do you hate me then?'

'No, I don't hate you.'

'Well then, if you don't hate me, you love me.'

Bhuqa was confident that he could talk the girl into a corner from which she could not escape. He had more experience of this sort of situation than she had and knew just what to say and do. He could not be beaten by a girl when he had such a good chance. They were practically alone at the river. Anyone who saw them together would be convinced that they were lovers and had planned their meeting. It would be a disgrace to fail. There was no one to assist her. There was no bush to which she might run and hide. He felt that Zuziwe could not resist that last argument, and that all she could do was to look down shyly. But Zuziwe was cool and confident as she answered him and repulsed that last statement.

'Don't be so fast, man,' she replied. 'I didn't say I love you.'

'Don't you like me just a little, Zuziwe?'

'Yes, Bhuqa, I like you.'

'Won't you consent, then, to be mine? I offer you all my love. Surely you can find it in your heart to say you will be mine, hoping you will grow to love me as we get to know each other better. Just try me, that's all. You won't be disappointed. I'm not one of those weak, watery, insipid men who don't deserve to be called men. I'm a real man, I am. Try me. That's all I ask.'

'No, Bhuqa, I cannot consent to be yours.'

'Why? What's your reason? Search your heart. Your reason for refusing to accept me may prove to be weak if examined carefully.'

Then a thought disturbed Bhuqa.

'Is there perhaps someone else you are in love with?' he asked in a cold voice.

'Yes,' replied Zuziwe, feeling that she must speak the truth, unpleasant though it must be to her companion. 'I am in love with a Hlubi man. Do you think there can be a girl of my age today who is not in love? I'm quite certain you too are in love with a girl, or possibly two or three girls, at the Thembu village. Right or wrong?'

'It's not with girls as it is with boys. Surely you must see that?'

'What do you mean? Do girls not feel as jealous as boys, or even more jealous, when their lovers are unfaithful? By what right do boys have an affair with more than one girl and then condemn girls when they do the same? No, boy, if ever I became your girl and discovered that you were having an affair with another girl, I should make things so hot for you that you would wish me at the bottom of the deepest pool of the Xesi river.'

'May I take this to be your consent that we become lovers?'

'Hayi, O no, be steady now. I didn't say so.'

'I thought you were consenting to be my girl on this condition: that if I have many girls, you will collect many boys for yourself.'

'No, thank you. I don't accept that. My policy is: One girl, one boy. One boy, one girl. That's the dish that agrees with me.'

'I like your dish. May I taste it now?'

With these words Bhuqa moved closer, took Zuziwe by the hand and tried to kiss her on the mouth. Zuziwe turned her face to one side to avoid the kiss and pushed him gently back.

'You are faster than lightning, aren't you?' she observed. 'Please give me time to think this over.'

'When will you give me your answer?'

'In a week or two,' replied Zuziwe evasively.

'Where and when shall I meet you?' persisted Bhuqa. 'You know it's not easy for me to meet you. Will you come to the river at about this time next week?'

'No, Bhuqa, that won't do,' replied Zuziwe. 'There may be other girls when I come to the river, and then I shall not get the opportunity to speak to you privately. I think I can arrange to visit my malume at your village either next week or the week after. Then it will be easy for me to meet you and give you my answer.'

'Dearest Zuziwe,' said Bhuqa, in an appealing tone,

'I hope it will be the answer I want. Promise me it will be a good answer.'

There was a soft look in Zuziwe's eyes as she gazed into his eyes, and her face wore a smile like sunshine. She felt a gush of love for Bhuqa. He stirred in her a passion which her lover, Ntabeni, was incapable of rousing. She felt it in her heart, in her mind, in her stomach, in every part of her body. Something warned her that their love was likely to be deep and dangerous, and her passion as irresistible as the current of the Xesi river when in flood. Only traditional modesty prevented her from accepting Bhuqa's love there and then. She was also saved by the arrival of four other girls from her village. After exchanging the customary greetings with the girls, and meaningful glances with Zuziwe, Bhuqa crossed the river by the bridge of stones and went back to his village. The girls who had just arrived were curious. They wanted to know what Zuziwe and Bhuqa had been talking about. Zuziwe tried to evade their searching questions and keen glances by answering carelessly. But it was not easy to do this. One girl, named Nomi Nqwelo, accused her pointedly.

'I saw you two before you saw us, Zuziwe. You were looking deep into each other's eyes. What was this that was so interesting? I didn't know you to be such a close friend of that Thembu boy.'

'There was nothing interesting at all. I have met Bhuqa during my visits to my uncle.' Zuziwe tried to be casual in her explanation. 'His sister, Notizi, is an intimate friend of mine. We were talking about her all the time.'

'Girl, we are not babies,' cut in Ntombi Dakada, a

blear-eyed, sour-faced, starved-looking girl. 'You can't fool us so easily. There's something between you and that Thembu boy. And I shall not have it, Zuziwe; no, I shall not. Ntabeni is my cousin. I shall not stand by and see him fooled by the whore that you are. I want a clean, pure wife for my cousin, not a deep, dirty, over-used thing, a convenient cesspool for any man who wants to relieve himself.'

'What language is this? Why do you insult me, Ntombi? What have I done that you should speak to me like this?'

'You know what you have done, you dirty slut,' Ntombi hissed at her. She had never liked Zuziwe, whose beautiful face and shapely figure always made her feel bitter that she had uneven features, bow legs, flat breasts and coarse skin. Her suppressed bitterness erupted today and she poured it out. 'If you are determined to give yourself to every boy who lifts his eyes in your direction, then you should stop tempting Ntabeni. I won't have it. No, I simply won't have it.'

As she said these words Ntombi moved closer and spat into Zuziwe's face. Zuziwe, stung by the insults, tried to spit back. Ntombi jumped nimbly out of the way of the spray of saliva and moved in to pommel Zuziwe with her fists. Zuziwe was no fighter. She tried to hit blindly at Ntombi, who skilfully warded off the blows and landed clever blows on the face and breasts and stomach of the unfortunate girl. The other girls looked on, enjoying the one-sided fight. Their jealousy had filled them with hatred of Zuziwe and this was the day of their vengeance. After a time one of them, either out of pity or because she could not laugh any more, moved in and held Ntombi back.

'Ndiyeke,' shouted Ntombi in a passion of anger. 'Let me

spoil the bitch's face. I want her to be as ugly as I am from today. Let me flatten her breasts. Perhaps that Thembu boy has put a child into that big stomach of hers. Let me flatten the belly and force an abortion lest it be thought the child is Ntabeni's.'

With these words Ntombi gave Zuziwe a violent push backwards, and the unhappy girl fell on her back into a deep pool of water at the river's edge. Zuziwe panicked. She beat the water with her hands in an effort to save herself from drowning. Fortunately, the river was not too deep at this spot, and when her feet touched the bottom, she stood up and was able to keep her head above the water. She waded to the river's edge and tried to scramble up the bank. She found the bank slippery, and when she was about to reach dry ground, she lost her foothold and fell back with a splash, adding to the enjoyment and mocking laughter of the other girls. She tried a drier spot. But when she was about to reach safe ground, one of the girls, the same girl who had rescued her from Ntombi's fists, approached her like one offering to help her. Poor Zuziwe held out her hand gratefully. The girl gave her a rough shove on the nose, and Zuziwe fell back into the water with a louder splash. Zuziwe's tormentors laughed until the tears came out of their eyes. Ntombi laughed until her stomach ached, and her legs became so weak that she could not stand on them but sprawled on the ground and rolled over from side to side. She could not stop laughing. It had gone beyond ordinary laughter and had become a sort of madness. Her mocking laughter hurt Zuziwe more than the blows she had received. She realized that her tormentors' hatred of her was so strong that they would continue to persecute her. She decided to cross over to the opposite side of the river, and thus put a good distance between herself and them. If they followed her, then she would have to go to her malume's home in the Thembu village, explain everything, and ask for an escort back home.

Fortunately, there was no need to do this. Her tormentors had had enough fun for the day. Apart from an occasional shout of derision, they paid no attention to her. They entered the shallow part of the river, washed and rubbed their feet vigorously on the grey round stones, pulled up their skirts almost to the point of exposing themselves, and washed as much of their bodies as could be reached without actually stripping naked. Then they filled their buckets with clean water higher up the river, balanced them on their heads, and walked back to Kwazidenge village.

Zuziwe sat on the bank of the river for a long time. Tears were pouring down from her eyes. Her heart was bleeding. She felt humiliated by the insults and the assault, and was troubled by the threat to her love for Bhuqa. She looked through her tears at the current of the river without actually seeing it. After a time she noticed that two distinct currents came from the two sides of the island higher up the river and met at a point opposite the spot where she sat. The course of each current was smooth and even, but when they met, their flow was arrested and their progress disturbed. Then they reorganized themselves and formed a bigger, stronger current which flowed down smoothly again. The current moved on in one single sheet of water. Then it curved smoothly and noiselessly over an uneven shelf of rock, and when it landed at the bottom of the shelf, it broke up into a chaos of foam and noise, and into minute splashes of water which were tossed high up into the air. Zuziwe noted that the water gathered itself together again below the fall and moved on in a steady, motionless mass towards its destiny. She knew that it was destined to pass through other rapids, other falls, till it reached the mighty ocean far away. After that it would probably ascend to the heavens above to begin the everlasting cycle all over again. Zuziwe watched, fascinated. Her contemplation of the eddies and the splashes and the chaos in the current of the river gradually brought peace and quiet into her own soul and stilled the strong currents of feeling which had rioted inside her body. Her grief was dulled, and the tears stopped flowing.

Two of the little girls who had been swimming and playing in the river and had seen the unequal fight approached Zuziwe to offer help. They saw the distress which still showed in her face and hesitated. Zuziwe lifted up her eyes and saw the expression of concern and fear in their faces. She spoke to them in a calm voice.

'What is it, girls, what do you want?' she asked.

'Nothing, sis' Zuziwe. We would like to help you if we can. May we fill your bucket with water?'

'No, girls, it's too big for you. You won't be able to lift it out of the water when it's full. I'll do it myself. Don't worry. I'll soon be all right.'

'Why did those girls attack you, sisi?'

'I really don't know.'

'They are such cowards. Four of them against one. Did you quarrel with them at the village?'

'No, girls, I too don't know why they attacked me. I've not quarrelled with them at any time, not even with Ntombi, the thin one who hit me with her fists.'

'She's just a collection of bones, that thing. How I hate her. Why didn't you take her with your hands and break her into two pieces? I'm sure you are much stronger than she is.'

'I'm not really a fighter, girls. I have always avoided fighting. I hate it. I think it's so stupid to fight, so pointless. You achieve nothing with it. When you fight you make worse what you are trying to put right. And the fighting never ends, once you rely on it to solve problems. Only fools fight. You know, this is the first fight I've ever been involved in. I hope it's the last.'

'But, sis' Zuziwe, fighting is the only language some people understand. If they discover you are a coward, they make you their plaything. But if they know you are a fighter, they leave you alone.'

'Well, people are not all the same. I hate fighting. Today's experience will not make me like it.'

The little girls, young as they were, were impressed by the fact that it was not cowardice but conviction which made Zuziwe declare her hatred of fighting and they respected her for it. They left her alone with her grief and went back to their own business of enjoying themselves, playing and swimming in the river with complete self-abandon as if there were no misery in the world.

II | *The Consequence*

Zuziwe arrived home late. Her parents were already feeling uneasy. A small boy from a neighbouring home had been sent by Duma, Zuziwe's eldest brother, to go down the road leading to the river to find out what had gone wrong.

'Zuziwe is coming along with Mlenzana of msenge section,' the boy had reported when he returned. 'I think there's something wrong. Zuziwe looks upset. She didn't speak when I told her you are worried that she is so late.'

'Is it Mlenzana who is delaying my child?' growled old Langa. 'Is he too becoming a rogue? What's this village coming to?'

'I don't think Mlenzana would delay Zuziwe,' said Mrs Langa. 'He's one of the best boys in the village. He is more likely to have helped her, whatever her trouble was.'

Zuziwe and Mlenzana arrived. Mlenzana helped Zuziwe to lift down the bucket of water from her head. Her father spoke to her in an angry voice.

'Why have you delayed at the river, Zuziwe?' he asked. Instead of answering, Zuziwe burst into a flood of tears.

'What's wrong, Zuziwe, my child?' asked her mother, with concern in her voice. 'What has happened to my child? Mlenzana, what has gone wrong?'

'I don't know the full story, mama,' replied Mlenzana.

'I got bits of it here and there, from Zuziwe's broken replies to the questions I asked her.'

'Where did you meet her?' asked Duma. 'Tell us what you know. And when Zuziwe has grown calm, she'll tell us the full story.'

'I was sitting on a large stone near the road that leads to the river when I heard a few girls approaching from the river, talking and laughing noisily. I was completely hidden from the road. As they came nearer, I heard what they said and realized that they were laughing over a fight they had had with Zuziwe. After they had passed I went down to the river. I saw Zuziwe on the far side of the river, on the Thembu side, with two little Thembu girls moving away from her. I shouted to her to cross the river and come and join me. At first she ignored me. Then she waved me off. But I insisted, shouting as hard as I could above the noise of the river. I told her it was growing late and that she should go home. After a time she crossed over. I helped her to fill up her bucket with water and put it on her head. Then I came back to the village with her. That's all I know about the affair.'

'Did she say nothing at all when you asked her about the fight?' asked Duma.

'Whenever she tried to speak, her words became indistinct. She ended up weeping. I thought it best to stop asking her about the events at the river and spoke to her about other things.'

'Who are the girls who did this?' asked Duma in a quiet voice which concealed the growing anger inside him. 'How many were they?'

'Zuziwe told me there were four of them,' replied Mlenzana, slowly, preferring to answer the second question first. 'I didn't see them because I was behind a rock when they passed me.'

'Could you not recognize them by their voices?' asked Duma again.

'I thought I recognized one voice as belonging to Ntombi Dakada of isinga section. It was a wheezy voice and I heard it more often than the others.'

'What about those other voices? Whose were they? Surely you grew up in this village? You know all the children of this village as well as I do.' Duma felt that Mlenzana was trying to shield the savages. His anger was rising against Mlenzana at what he took for cowardice. But Mlenzana was no coward. He did not fear to stand up boldly for the truth when it was necessary to do so.

'No, bhut' Duma,' he said in a calm voice. 'I see you don't understand. I'm not willing to identify the girls by their voices alone. I can't swear even to the wheezy voice and say it was definitely Ntombi's. There must be people who saw these girls and can testify that they assaulted Zuziwe. Or you could wait until you hear the full story from Zuziwe herself.'

'I am ready to tell it now,' said Zuziwe. She was speaking from her mother's breast in which she had buried her face. She lifted up her head and opened her eyes, which were still red with tears. 'I'll tell you everything, bhut' Duma. I think I'm feeling better now. First let me thank you, Mlenzana, with all my heart, for your kindness and help. Don't lose patience with him, bhut' Duma. You ought to thank him for helping me out of a difficult situation. As I sat on the river bank, on Thembu soil, I thought I might not reach home tonight. I thought those terrible girls were still waiting for me. I'm quite convinced that they wanted to kill me.'

Everybody in the room was shocked at these words.

Zuziwe's mother shouted above the exclamations of the others. 'Zuziwe, don't use such wild words,' she said. 'How could anyone wish to kill my baby?'

'Yes, mama, I could see murder in their eyes. Perhaps my helplessness, my inability to fight, brought out the brute in them. They must have hated me for something, though I can't say what it is.'

'You are not telling us the story clearly, Zuziwe,' interrupted her father. 'Try to give us a detailed account of the assault.'

'Excuse me, tata, my mind is confused. But I shall try to do so. I went down to the river to fetch water, as you know. I was alone. I sat on a large flat stone in the river and watched a group of small boys and girls playing and swimming in the river pool. Bhuqa of the Thembu village came and spoke to me.'

Duma's eyes flashed when Zuziwe mentioned Bhuqa's name. Zuziwe noticed this and hesitated.

'Did you allow that Thembu boy to sit and talk to you?' asked Duma. 'For how long did he sit with you?'

'I can't say,' replied Zuziwe, a little upset by Duma's hostile attitude. 'We talked for some time.'

'Don't disturb her, Duma,' said old Langa. 'Allow her to tell her story and ask questions at the end.'

'All right, Zuziwe, go on,' replied Duma. But it was clear that all was not right.

Zuziwe went on. 'As Bhuqa was about to leave, four girls from our village came. They were Ntombi Dakada, Nomi Nqwelo, Makaziwe Godlwana and Nompongo Sophunga, all from isinga section. Bhuqa went away when they came.'

'Why?' asked Duma again. 'Was he feeling guilty?'

'No, bhuti, it wasn't guilt,' replied Zuziwe. 'He was about to go when the girls came.'

'I see. It's strange that he should be so keen to go away when those girls came. However, go on with your story.'

'The girls were as suspicious as my brother is. They said I had been flirting with Bhuqa. They insulted me, using very abusive language. Ntombi accused me of being unfaithful to her cousin, Ntabeni.'

'She was quite right too,' interrupted Duma again, now quite angry. 'I'm ashamed that my own sister was caught showing favour to a cursed Thembu boy.'

'She insulted me, bhut' Duma. I'm sure you won't be so ready to agree with her when you hear what she said. She called me a whore, the cesspool of men. Then she attacked me, hit me on my stomach, saying she believed that Bhuqa had made me pregnant and that she wanted to force an abortion.'

Old Langa stood up, took his black, oiled msimbithi stick, and called on Duma, Mlenzana and Zuziwe to go with him to Ntombi's home. Duma objected.

'Mlenzana is a boy, bawo. Why do you want us to go with an uncircumcized boy to discuss this? Where are the men of the village?'

'You speak like a child, Duma, with very little knowledge, though you think you are wise. I am not now going to the village court to lay a charge. I am going to Ntombi's father to discuss this with him as head of his family. Remember that the Dakadas and the Mlilos are one family. Ntabeni Mlilo will soon be Zuziwe's husband. Mlenzana is coming along with us as an eyewitness. Besides, boys are often called upon to give evidence, even at the village court. Come, we waste time and it will soon grow dark.'

From the eminence of the Langa home the group went down a narrow path in single file. They crossed the dry Bonkolo brook and walked for some time till they reached the huts where the Dakadas lived in isinga section. The view from the Dakada home was poor. The distant Bhukazana peak of the Mathole range of mountains could not be seen. The only view to the west and the south was the Hill of Fools, with mud huts scattered on the hillside like dark-brown pimples on a pale-brown face. To the east and the north the view of the landscape was obscured by a thick cluster of mimosa trees.

As Mvangeli Langa and his group were approaching their destination, they were greeted by the barking of several dogs. The fury of the dogs grew as the four reached the huts. A young man, Zisani Dakada, came out of one of the huts. When he saw the visitors, he tried unsuccessfully to calm the dogs. He was forced after some time to pick up a few stones to throw at them. Those he hit ran away, yelling with pain, while those he missed continued to bark furiously, but at a respectful distance from the stonethrower. The four visitors kept a dignified, calm air during this noisy welcome; but the men were ready with their sticks, and they kept the girl in the middle. They reached the large hut in which visitors were received. Duma knocked and a strong, deep voice bade them enter.

'Greetings, Ndlovu,' said old Langa on behalf of his party.

'Greetings, Bhele,' replied Dakada, father of Zisani and Ntombi. 'You and your son may sit on the bench. You are not too stout to share it and be comfortable. Your daughter may sit on the mat near the fireplace. Let the boy squat near the door, or join the other boys round the fire near the cattle-kraal.'

'No, no, hayi, myeke, Ndlovu. We have come here on special business and we need him here. Thank you all the same, Ndlovu. We are quite comfortable. Zuziwe likes to sit near the fire. She'll be very comfortable where she is.'

'What has brought you here so late, Bhele? asked Dakada lightly, but with watchful eyes. 'It must be very important business to tear you away from your favourite task of counting and inspecting your cattle when they return to the kraal.'

'Ewe, Ndlovu, it is rather serious,' replied Mvangeli. Then, after a short pause, he plunged into the business like a diver jumping into a swimming pool. 'Your daughter and three other girls attacked my daughter at the Xesi river this afternoon. She insulted Zuziwe, using very bad language. As we shall soon be connected through the children if all goes well, I decided to come at once so that we may find out more about the trouble and settle it together.'

'I'm sorry to hear this, Bhele, extremely sorry. This is very painful to me. My daughter returned from the river some time ago, after a long delay. It was growing late and she still had to go and gather wood at the sinquma woodland on the other side of the hill. I don't think she's back yet, but I shall send for her.'

Dakada left the hut, called his wife, Mamtolo, to tell her of Langa's complaint, and ordered her to send for Ntombi at once. Then he returned to the visitors. After a short time his wife also entered the hut. Dakada introduced the subject again. Mamtolo listened with a tense, disturbing quietness, her eyes fixed on old Langa or Zuziwe or Mlenzana, but never on her husband, even when he was speaking.

'While we are waiting for Ntombi to come,' said Dakada, 'will the girl or any of you tell us what happened and who caused the fight?'

'I think Mlenzana who knows more about this than I, and my son should speak first so as to spare Zuziwe's feelings. She has suffered enough already. She can fill the gaps left by Mlenzana when he has finished. Or she can answer questions put to her directly.'

Mamtolo's eyes had been flashing fire during Langa's speech, and as soon as he stopped speaking, she burst out in a harsh voice and with an ugly sneer on her face.

'Why did you bring the girl, then,' she asked, 'if your purpose is to shield her? Or is it that you fear she will blunder into the truth and show herself up as the troublemaker?'

'Mamtolo, thula!' said Dakada sharply. 'I'm handling this. I called you in that you may hear for yourself what your daughter is accused of. You may ask questions when you have heard the full story. If you behave like a foolish woman and judge before you have heard the facts, or if you speak out of turn, I'll send you out.'

'I will not keep quiet when false things are said about my child,' answered Mamtolo stubbornly. 'I alone bore the pangs of birth for this child. I cleaned her and washed her napkins when she dirtied herself. I kept awake and nursed her through the night when she cried because of stomach ache or fever. I took her to the doctor when she was very ill and in danger of dying. Let no one tell me to keep quiet when my baby is being persecuted.'

'Mamtolo, keep quiet, at once, or I take you out,' Dakada thundered at her.

Mamtolo fumed and snorted. But after a threatening look from her husband, who half rose from his seat, she kept quiet, submitting herself rather angrily to him. The men had to be satisfied. Mlenzana was called upon to speak. He described all the events as he had seen them. It grew darker and darker in the room, and Mamtolo fetched a paraffin tin lamp, which she lit and placed in front of her husband. Its light was weak and it gave off a heavy paraffin odour and a cloud of smoke as thick as that of a witch's cauldron. The combined light of the lamp and the fire was feeble. It made all the people inside the room look grim. Mamtolo lingered like a witch in the gloom at the back of the hut. Her eyes glowed like the baleful eyes of a cat. She cast an evil atmosphere on the proceedings and made father Langa despair of achieving his purpose of promoting peace and good relations between the two families.

Zuziwe was fascinated by Dakada's shadow, cast on the curved mud wall of the hut by the feeble light of the lamp. In the shadow he appeared larger than life. The shadow exaggerated his movements and his gestures, the nodding or shaking of his head, the opening and shutting of the mouth as he spoke, till Zuziwe felt as if he were one of those fabulous giants she had so often been told about by her late grandmother, which had superhuman powers, a superhuman sense of sight and of smell and of hearing, powers which they often used to destroy ordinary human beings. Would he act like one of the inhuman monsters or would he be like one of the rarer type, the good giants who rescued people from the clutches of the cruel ones?

Zisani was ordered to go and meet Ntombi and tell her to hurry up. As he stepped outside, a dog barked near the cattle-kraal. Other dogs came out and rushed up to the scene of the disturbance, barking too. Zisani went to the kraal to investigate. A cat was sitting on a top branch of an old tree-trunk a few yards from the kraal entrance. It was watching the dogs, making no sound, no movement. The dogs barked more and more furiously. Some tried to jump up at the cat. But they failed by a few feet each time. The cat was safe from danger as long as it remained calm and kept its wits. What the source of the dogs' anger was, it was difficult to say. The cat had not interfered with them. But every member of the dog community in the neighbourhood responded to the call to battle, and a large contingent of dogs gathered at the battlefield and joined in the fight that was no fight. But alas, as the company of dogs grew larger and larger, and the barking more and more furious and frightening, the cat lost its nerve. It misjudged the position and took the wrong decision. It thought that the man approaching was on its side and was trying to restrain the dogs. What led to its error of judgement was that the dogs avoided the side on which Zisani was standing, shouting and throwing stones. The cat decided there was an opening on this side. It jumped down, streaked off close to the man, hoping to make for the roof tops. It would have made its escape, had it not been for two latecomers of the dog company which suddenly appeared in front of it. The front dog dashed towards the cat, grabbed, missed. The other dog caught the cat by the tail and the circle of dogs closed in. In desperation, and screaming worse than sinners in hell, the cat turned round and tried to fight. It hit out with its paws and bit with its teeth. But it was hopeless. Its courage could not prevail against the heavy odds opposing it. The dogs grabbed each of the cat's four legs. One held it by the throat. Another sank its teeth into its soft belly. In a short time they had pulled it to pieces, ignoring Zisani's efforts to beat them off. The dogs seemed to have gone mad with hate and the urge to kill.

When the cat was dead, the dogs left, returned to their homes and went about their daily business as if nothing had happened. They were not in the least interested in the carcass. They had not attacked the cat because they wanted food to eat, but because the instinct to kill had been roused and had grown into a force as terrible, as irresistible, as destructive as the raging torrent of the Xesi river when it overflows its banks.

Before the drama of the cat and the dogs was played out, Ntombi and her companions arrived. They stood a little distance away, watching, half frightened, half fascinated, each with a load of firewood balanced on her head. They watched as the little girls and boys had watched Ntombi pommel and batter Zuziwe at the river. Zisani spoke to Ntombi and told her about the four visitors from beyond Bonkolo brook, and the purpose of their visit. She must appear before her father and the visitors as soon as she had put down her bundle of firewood. Ntombi obeyed at once and was soon in the hut. At first she tried to deny that she was the aggressor. She made a counter-accusation against Zuziwe, alleging that it was Zuziwe who swore at her when she accused her of being unfaithful to her cousin, Ntabeni. Ntombi explained that she was stung by her curses and swore back at her. Zuziwe hit her on the nose with the back of her hand. Then they fought till they were parted by her friends.

'How did your friends part you?' asked Duma. 'Did they hold the hands of both of you, or did they come between you and push you off, or did they hit you to make you stop fighting, as is sometimes done?'

'I can't remember clearly,' replied Ntombi, suspecting a trap. 'I think they came between us but they didn't hold down our hands.'

'Did you both stop fighting when your companions tried to stop you?'

'I stopped at once,' replied Ntombi with more confidence, 'but Zuziwe forced her way past them and hit me in the face.'

'Can you show us a mark where she hit you?' asked Duma again, almost like a trained lawyer.

'No. I warded off her blows and hit her back,' replied Ntombi.

'So you cannot show just one single mark to prove that Zuziwe hit you, and yet she has marks to show she was hit all over the body, kicked on the stomach, and scratched on the face and neck. Her clothes were wet when she reached home. Does this not prove that her story is true when she says you pushed her into the water?'

'Are you accusing me of telling lies?' Ntombi flashed out angrily. 'Are you trying to shield this rotten sister of yours who is unfaithful to my cousin? Go on then, send her to that Thembu rogue and cut out all the pretence. After all she is always ready to lie on her back for a man. But she will not become Ntabeni's wife if she behaves so disgracefully!'

'I would rather not marry a man who has such a liar for a cousin,' Zuziwe broke in. 'My character and my behaviour are not your concern. I can look after myself well enough. I shall certainly not marry into a family where I shall be persecuted by ruffians who have failed to find husbands for themselves and then try to make the lives of other people worse than hell.'

Old Langa tried to intervene.

'Zuziwe, I don't want to hear another word from you,' he said. 'We have come to restore peace between our families, not to continue the fight which started down at the river. You must control yourself.'

'But, tata, how can I control myself when this girl tells so many lies and continues to insult me as she did at the river?'

'*Hulekazindini!* You slut! I dare you to become Ntabeni's wife for just one week. You'll be taught how to behave. Our family is not to be trifled with. The beating I gave you at the river is nothing compared to what you'll get if you don't behave properly.'

Dakada suddenly roared out in a loud voice: 'Ntombi!'

All became silent. Ntombi looked with eyes full of fear at her father, but with angry eyes at Zuziwe.

'Ntombi,' said Dakada again, but in a quieter voice, 'if you say another word, I shall end all this talking and give you a thorough beating. Speak only when you are spoken to, and answer the questions you are asked.'

It was all quiet but for Zuziwe's sobbing. She was ashamed of her tears. They were tears of anger mixed with tears of anxiety at the threat to her love for Bhuqa, a threat she had seen not only in Ntombi but also in her brother, Duma. It became clear to her that she loved Bhuqa with a love that brought a stinging pain into the pit of her stomach. So the tears came down like a flood after a heavy shower of rain. Her father, noticing the tears, decided that the time had come to end the meeting. He appealed to Dakada.

'Ndlovu, we have spoken on this unfortunate incident long enough. We have heard both sides of the affair, and that was our purpose in coming here. A quarrel between our families should be avoided. I'm not interested in trying to decide who was wrong. That is likely to be a difficult task which will probably take the whole night; and in the end we may find that we have decided the case but have failed to promote friendship between our families. Good relations and real friendship are very important between neighbours, friends and relatives if life is to be worthwhile.'

'Bhele, I thank you for your good words,' said Dakada, in a firm voice which revealed quiet determination. 'They do you credit indeed. But I cannot accept them. It is clear from the statements made by the two girls that my daughter was the troublemaker. It's generous of you to suggest that we should not punish the offender, but it would be mean of me to accept that suggestion knowing as I do that your daughter has suffered injury. My child must be punished now, in your presence, in this very room. I have my sjambok here.

Your daughter, Mlenzana, Zisani and my wife will leave the room. But you and your son must stay and see justice done on my child. I am a man of peace. But peace without fairness and justice is a hollow mockery. Is that not true, Bhele?'

'There is truth in your words, Ndlovu,' replied Mvangeli. 'But you must remember that justice without mercy is very much like tyranny. And so I beg you to be merciful, to forgive and forget.'

'Your words are good again, Bhele,' replied Dakada. 'Their flavour is good. But mercy follows repentance. There's no sign of repentance in my daughter. I don't think she is troubled by what she has done.'

'Perhaps she'll ask to be forgiven if she's given a chance now,' said Mvangeli, rather doubtfully.

All eyes turned towards Ntombi, but she kept her face averted and did not speak. Her whole body, hard as a wall of granite, reflected her unyielding and unbending obstinacy. Her mother spoke defiantly from the dark corner where she sat in the shadow cast by Dakada's body.

'I'll not allow you to torment my child,' she said. 'Why should she ask for forgiveness? Let no one touch my child, I warn you. You call yourself her father and yet you take sides against her. You should be ashamed of yourself. You should be her protector, not her tormentor. I'll not sit by and allow you to assault my child. You'll have to destroy me first.'

'Woman, go to your hut,' Dakada shouted. Mamtolo sat stubbornly on the floor. Dakada rose, grabbed her by the right arm, and half pulled, half led her out. Mamtolo followed, half yielding, half resisting.

After a short while Dakada returned and asked Mlenzana,

Zisani and Zuziwe to leave the room. He threw down the blanket which he had wrapped round the upper part of his body like a cloak and stood erect in vest and trousers. He took down his sjambok from a hook in the wall and tried it out once or twice by hitting the air. Then he slowly approached Ntombi, called her by name and asked her one or two questions to work himself up to the right mood.

'Ntombi,' he said, 'do you admit that you attacked this Langa girl unprovoked?'

No answer.

'Do you realize that you behaved disgracefully, and that you have lowered your family in the eyes of the village?'

Still no answer.

Ntombi's resistance was so hard that the men could almost feel it cut them and lower their status as men and their authority in the community. Mvangeli wished to intervene and to appeal to Dakada not to inflict corporal punishment on his daughter, but he was hardened by her stubbornness and did not intervene. Ntombi's obstinacy was a manifestation of her hatred of Zuziwe and of her anger because the men were trying to cancel out the punishment she had given to the girl. She was not really angry with the men; she merely blamed them for making fools of themselves by allowing Zuziwe to use them as her instruments. Even now she felt she would gladly do anything that would give Zuziwe physical or mental pain.

So she sat with averted face. Dakada lifted the sjambok high up and brought it down hard on Ntombi's left thigh. Ntombi's body tightened. Dakada hit her three more times, but there was still no reaction. Then he lost his temper and hit her all over the body in a frenzy of anger. Mamtolo rushed into the hut, shouting and cursing like an escaped demon from hell, and threw herself on Dakada to hold him back. Dakada pushed her away with his left hand, gave her two blows on her thighs, turned round and continued hitting his daughter. Mother and daughter broke into howls and shrieks, like witches in torment, as if the end of the world had come. Mamtolo threw herself on Ntombi and tried to shield her by covering her body with her own. Dakada hit on, not caring whether the blows landed on mother or daughter, until Mvangeli and Duma held him back, giving the women a chance to escape.

Mvangeli spoke to Dakada, pleading with him. '*Kwanele*, it's enough, Ndlovu, it's enough. If you go on hitting that child you'll hurt her and there'll be trouble. You may even find yourself under arrest.'

'Under arrest!' Dakada yelled at him. 'I should like to see the policeman that will dare arrest me and the magistrate that will convict me for teaching my own daughter how to behave.'

'You speak these words in anger, my friend,' replied Mvangeli. 'The law doesn't permit a man to use a sjambok excessively, even on his own daughter. You don't have to use violence to make a good woman of your daughter. And you have no right to hit your wife. You should have held back when she fell on the girl to shield her. The punishment you have given is more than enough now, even for your stubborn daughter.'

'Daughter!' Dakada yelled again. 'That's no daughter of

mine. That's a devil straight from hell. She is full of evil. I would have done well to have destroyed her altogether.'

'No, Ndlovu,' replied the older man gently. 'Do not speak words in anger which you'll regret afterwards. I'm quite certain that Ntombi has learnt her lesson despite her stubbornness. It's good that she melted and cried. Let us be satisfied and hope that this has helped to purge her of evil.'

Dakada was not convinced, but eventually he submitted to the older man. In fact, he had no choice. He could not continue hitting mother and daughter indefinitely. On calmer reflection the irony of the situation struck him. He realized that he had resorted to violence to prevent violence. What he had meted out was not normal punishment. It was violent assault. His aim was right but the execution of it was wrong. He had to admit that it was hard for a man to be wise when he was roused to a fury of anger by a mere chit of a girl. It was harder if she was his own daughter, for her wickedness was an indirect accusation of him, an indication of his inability to bring up his children properly, a betrayal of an evil streak in the parents, whose blood ran in her veins.

The incident left an acid taste in Dakada's mouth. After seeing his visitors off, he went to his hut, which he found empty, for his wife was trying to comfort his daughter in the maidens' hut. So he spread out his grass mat, lay down on it, covered himself with two blankets and tried to sleep. But sleep would not come. He lay awake for several hours, and still his wife did not come. It was not until after the cocks began to crow that he fell asleep.

III | *At Home*

It was with a sense of relief that Zuziwe and Mlenzana came out of the visitors' hut. Their homes lay in opposite directions, but as it was quite dark, and Zuziwe was afraid to cross Bonkolo brook alone, Mlenzana offered to escort her home. But even in Mlenzana's company the sounds and shadows of the night frightened Zuziwe. As they were crossing the brook, the frogs suddenly burst into the most unmusical chorus ever heard. Mlenzana assured Zuziwe that there was nothing to fear from the frogs and the night. As they were moving up the narrow path leading to her home, Zuziwe's heart beat faster, and then she saw a person moving in front of them. She drew Mlenzana's attention to the person. He laughed at her and told her it was a shrub which gave the impression that it was moving because she was moving. As they approached the garden in front of her home, Zuziwe was startled by an owl which suddenly cried, 'Who! Who!', as if it was asking God whose turn it was to die next. This time she controlled herself and succeeded in hiding her fear. Mlenzana escorted her right up to the door of the cottage and did not leave her until her mother opened the door and she was safely inside.

'Mama, aren't you in bed yet?' said Zuziwe as she greeted her mother.

'I couldn't go to bed before you and your father returned,' replied her mother. 'Where's your father? And where's Duma?'

'We left them at tata Dakada's home. Mlenzana was kind enough to escort me home when he noticed that I was afraid of the night.'

'Would your father have been so thoughtless as to let you walk home alone at night?'

'No, mama. Tata knew that Mlenzana was there to take me halfway but he did, after all, bring me right to our door. Fortunately, we didn't meet any danger. I had my guardian angel looking after me,' replied Zuziwe. 'Where's everybody, mama? Are they off to bed?'

'They went off long ago. It's almost midnight. Here's your dish of mvubo. Sit down and eat. You must be hungry. I'm sure you were not offered even a drop of something to moisten your lips.'

'Thank you, mama,' replied Zuziwe gratefully. 'There was no chance to think of food at tata Dakada's home.'

'If your father and your brother don't return soon, I won't sit up any longer. Do tell me what happened. Did that wild girl admit her guilt?'

'No, mama, don't ask me to tell you what happened. Please wait for tata and ask him to tell you the whole story. It was terribly upsetting. I don't want to think of it tonight.'

'Why, baby, what happened? Did your father and your brother allow that girl to insult you right in their presence?'

'No, mama, don't blame tata or bhut' Duma. They themselves didn't know that Ntombi has such an evil temper. Tata Dakada was furious with his daughter and his wife.

Mrs Dakada is a bad woman, mama. But I don't know what happened after I left. Tata will tell you the full story.'

By this time Zuziwe had finished eating, though she could not eat more than half the food in her dish. The two women went to their rooms. Mvangeli and Duma returned soon after the women had undressed and tucked themselves up comfortably in their blankets. It was too late for the men to take time over their mvubo, a mixture of ground boiled corn and sour milk. They gobbled it down and went to bed without giving the food a chance to settle in the stomach. Mvangeli went to his bedroom and Duma went to the hut which he shared with his wife and three of his children, a few yards away from the cottage. Zuziwe slept in the second bedroom of the cottage, sharing it with two of Duma's eldest daughters.

Mama Langa was not asleep when her husband came in. She was curious to know all the details of the visit to Dakada's home.

'Father of Zuziwe,' she said, addressing him in the traditional manner (which enabled her to show respect and at the same time prevent the children from becoming too familiar with the name of the head of the family), 'why have you delayed so long? I couldn't sit up any longer. I thought you wouldn't come back tonight. Did you see your food on the table?'

'Yes, thank you, we have eaten it already,' replied her husband. 'We delayed because Dakada asked us to stay and see him punish his daughter. He was very angry with her. I had to restrain him for fear that he might hurt her.'

'I hope it has taught her a lesson,' said Mrs Langa. 'Some

of these girls learn rough tricks in the big towns and bring them to our village.'

'Your son, Duma, is very angry with Zuziwe. He feels that she encouraged that Thembu boy.'

'Duma is stupid. What did he expect Zuziwe to do when a boy she knows came and spoke to her? Did he expect her to be rude and refuse to speak to him and chase him away from her? The river was made by God to flow where it flows and nobody has the right to chase another person away from it. Really, Duma is stupid. I have no patience with him.'

Mvangeli finished undressing. He blew out the candle and joined his wife in bed. He was soon asleep. But his wife lay awake for some time, first lying on one side, then on the other, for sleep did not come easily to her. After a time she too fell asleep, and her gentle snores made an untuneful accompaniment to her husband's deep, guttural, discordant snores which sounded much like a motor-car engine missing fire.

Early next morning the whole family gathered in the living-room for morning worship. Evening worship had not been held on the previous day because of the disturbance to the daily routine. In the absence of her husband Mrs Langa had merely knelt down with her grandchildren and prayed, and had made them say the Lord's prayer. So today, morning worship was held for all the members of the family.

Mvangeli took a hymn book, thumbed through it for a while, and then decided on a hymn. He read through the hymn very fast, like an auctioneer who has warmed up to his job. He paused for a second or two, like a diver about to plunge into the deep waters of the Xesi river. Then he burst out singing in his deep powerful voice, and was immediately joined by the other members of the family. Zuziwe and Duma's wife sang soprano, their rich, full voices blending well. Mrs Langa assisted another daughter-in-law who was singing alto, but sometimes she left her alone and went to the assistance of Duma, who was struggling to sing tenor. It was a delightful performance. Even the weak, flat voices of the untalented members of the family served as a background to the singing of the four gifted singers and added something to the melody.

And so the hymn was sung. All of it. Not one of its eight verses was left out. Mvangeli even stretched it out by leading his family choir to repeat the last verse. Then the 'Amen' was sung and its echoes passed out into the sun-bathed valley and slope of the Hill of Fools.

Mvangeli opened his Bible and turned to his favourite passage, the first psalm. He read slowly, paying careful attention to each sentence, and stressing those words which he felt were important. He did not comment. That was not the way of conducting family worship. But there was eloquent comment in the modulation of his voice and the expression of his eyes when he looked up. He read the last verse twice, to stress the promise and the warning in it: 'For the Lord knoweth the way of the righteous; but the way of the ungodly shall perish.' Then he shut the Bible with a bang, even before he had finished reading.

Prayer followed. There was moving of chairs and stools and a scraping noise on the bare wooden floor as everyone knelt down. Mvangeli called on his wife to pray by touching her on the shoulder. His wife knew by that sign what she was required to do. She prayed in a clear firm voice, like one who was experienced in praying out loud in the hearing of others. Her husband occasionally bellowed out an encouraging response.

Zuziwe did not attend to the prayer all the time. Her mind kept wandering to other matters which were nearer to her than the Bible characters whose experiences her mother was recounting, or the endless list of unfortunate people for whom everybody always prayed. She wondered whether Bhuqa, if she accepted him and married him, would be interested in the church, and whether they would observe the daily routine of morning and evening worship. She wondered how many homes were as particular on family worship as her home was. Does it make a person good, she wondered, to sing hymns and pray daily and go to church regularly? Does it make him better than those who neglect these things? Would her own father be a worse man if he did not pray so much? She knew her father to be patient, kind and generous. Would he be impatient, cruel and mean if he prayed less? Bhuqa too, from what she knew of him, had a good heart. But Zuziwe did not believe he would ever be particular about prayer and worship. Would he then change and become evil? There was no reason why he should. She herself did not wish to marry a man who was as keen on the church and family worship as her father was. She wanted to go to church only when she was in the mood for it and the preacher was interesting. How could anyone bear to have morning and evening worship every day of every year for the rest of one's life? Perhaps Ntabeni, who was keen on the church, would observe family worship strictly if he became her husband. But now it seemed unlikely that she would marry him. The intimacy that had grown between her and Bhuqa made her often wonder why she had consented to marry Ntabeni. She was only seventeen at that time, and was too immature to understand men, or to know what it was to be in love. Surely it had been unfair of Ntabeni to offer her marriage then, and of her brothers to press her to accept him? How could she be expected to judge wisely in her choice of a partner who would live with her for the rest of her life?

Zuziwe was disturbed in her thoughts and her mind was brought back to the prayer by a nudging contest which broke out between the children kneeling next to her. One child, growing tired of chewing his bubble-gum, had taken it out of his mouth and stuck it onto the sole of the shoe of the child next to him. The offended child had protested by nudging the offender, who had nudged back. Zuziwe pinched the arms of the two contestants. One of them expressed his protest at the severity of the punishment by emitting a suppressed yell. Duma gave the yelling youngster a sharp rap on the head with his kunckles, and the little boy had a better excuse for letting out a sharper yell. Mvangeli opened his eyes and glared at the children, and order was restored.

Mrs Langa prayed on. She prayed to God to give more of His attention to His people. Why was there so much hate between man and man, between family and family, between nation and nation? As God was omnipotent it was in His power to rid the world of these evils, to destroy the devil, to destroy sin and even death itself. The prayer came from a heart ravished with pain, Zuziwe thought. It was clear that her mother was tormented by the violent clashes between the Hlubis and the Thembus. Her prayer surely was not merely eloquence. She was distressed by the malice of people like Ntombi and the cruelty of boys like Diliza. Zuziwe wondered why God, who was all-powerful, allowed these things to happen. What was His purpose when He put into the mind of one person the will to hurt another person, to crack his skull, or knock out his eye, or rip open his belly? Why did He allow the first murderer, Cain, to plan and carry out the murder of a good, God-fearing man, his brother, Abel? Why did He not bring down an army of angels to protect that innocent young man who loved God and obeyed Him? Zuziwe was again called back to the prayer, but this time by the word 'amen' which ended it. Then the Lord's prayer was sung, with vigour and feeling, the benediction was pronounced, and morning worship ended.

Zuziwe set the table for breakfast, and Duma's wife went to the kitchen to dish out and serve food to the whole family. After breakfast Mvangeli went out to the fields to supervise the boys who were ploughing one of his plots. Mrs Langa attended to her grandchildren, feeding them, changing their napkins when necessary, and lulling them to sleep when they became fidgety. Duma saddled his horse, jumped on its back and galloped to town. Two herdboys drove the cattle into the fields which had been harvested and were now communal grazing fields. They took up positions between these fields and other fields which had not yet been harvested. They were joined a little later by other herdboys from the village.

Several tolofiya trees grew near the fields, and some of the boys went and plucked ripe, golden fruit from the trees. They wiped it carefully on the grass to remove the thorns. Then they cut it open with their fingernails and settled down to fill themselves with the delicious, juicy fruit. They had hardly eaten one pear each when Diliza Mququ, Katana Langa (Zuziwe's cousin) and one other boy of the warrior class arrived. Both Diliza and Katana were notorious bullies. They spread terror wherever they went and always left whining boys behind. When Diliza and his companions approached, the poor boys watched them with fear. Diliza saw their fear and spoke to them angrily.

'What's wrong with you, makwedini? Are you mad? Why do you look at us as if you are seeing ghosts? Have you done something wrong? Have you stolen this tolofiya?'

The boys trembled with fear and did not answer. This infuriated Diliza and he kicked the nearest boy, who rolled over, struggled to his feet and ran off. The other boys followed him, and Katana helped them to move faster by giving the boy nearest to him a sharp blow on the thigh with his mnquma stick. Then the three bullies sat down and ate the fruit. Diliza called back one youngster and ordered him to go and fetch water from Bonkolo brook. Katana told two boys to go to their homes and steal eggs. Others had to go and fetch sheaves from a haystack for the bullies to lie on and make themselves comfortable.

Diliza and his friends lay down on the ground, using the sheaves as pillows for their heads. After thirty minutes or so, they were disturbed in their rest by the voice of Zuziwe, who had come up to them thinking the two herdboys from her home were in the group.

'Molweni,' she said, and then looked at them in alarm when she saw her mistake. Diliza sat up and smiled.

'Molo, sithandwa,' he said, 'what have you brought us?'

'I've brought you nothing,' she replied as bravely as she could. 'I thought Sidodo was here. Do you know where he is?'

'No, Zuziwe, I don't know. Why do you worry about him? We are here.' Diliza stood up and walked slowly towards Zuziwe. She watched him and knew that he meant mischief. He inspected the dish of food which she was balancing on her head with her left hand, and the tin of amasi dangling in her right hand. He took the tin and was about to drink the milk when Zuziwe tried to stop him.

'This is my father's milk, Diliza,' she said. 'Please don't touch it.'

'Why do you bring it to us, if it's your father's? You can see your father isn't here. And for that matter I'm your father too. You can go back to your home and fetch more milk for that other father of yours who isn't here.'

With these words Diliza drank half the milk and gave the rest to his companions. Then he took the dish of food. It was a samp-and-bean mixture. Zuziwe tried to hold on to the dish, but Diliza wrenched it away from her and gave it to his friends.

'If I can't get you,' he said savagely, 'at least I can get your food. Do you remember what you said when we parted last time? I felt like going back to clap you on your mouth to make you shut up. I don't know why I didn't. Afterwards, do you know how I felt? I felt more and more angry every time I remembered your words. It's my turn today, and I mean to revenge myself for that insult. Sweet revenge. That's what it will be. Something to console me, to make me forget. You could enjoy it too. It could be sweet for both of us, if you care to make it so. Or are you so mad after that Thembu boy of yours that you cannot enjoy any other man? By the way, where is he, that Thembu boy? I hear you and Ntombi fought because of him.'

'Don't talk nonsense,' exclaimed Zuziwe angrily. 'I didn't fight for a boy, and I didn't fight Ntombi.'

'What did you do then? Did you embrace each other, you and Ntombi, down at the river? I wish I had gone down to the river that day, and not back to the village. I would have enjoyed meeting your boyfriend. Why didn't you tell me you had an appointment with him? I wouldn't have embraced him like you. A tap on the head with my stick would have put some sense into him. He would have learnt to leave Hlubi girls alone. Come, Zuziwe girl, do give me a taste of what you have reserved for Bhuqa.'

Diliza pulled Zuziwe violently towards him and tried to kiss her. She turned her head away and pushed him off. He tried again to kiss her on the mouth. They struggled and fell. The struggle continued on the ground. Diliza pinned her to the ground, kissed her violently on the mouth and would have raped her if his companions had not held him off.

The intervention of Diliza's friends helped Zuziwe to escape, leaving the dishes behind. She went home sobbing wretchedly. She told her mother about the assault. Her mother reported it to her father and her brothers when they arrived in the evening. Mvangeli had difficulty in restraining his sons, who took up their weapons with the intention of seeking out Diliza and assaulting him. They were held back by Mvangeli's promise to go to the headman next day to make a formal complaint against Diliza. But late that night Diliza's father, who had heard of the incident from his daughters, came to the home of the Langas to plead with Mvangeli not to take steps against his son. He offered reparation, even to the extent of paying a sheep for the assault. There had been many complaints against his son recently, the old man said. He feared that the headman would refuse to deal with the case and would pass it on to the magistrate's court. Attempted rape was a serious case. The punishment might be a jail sentence, and this would break him and his wife. He was planning to send the boy to the circumcision school, where he would be born again. It was necessary to make a man of him to put an end to his wild ways. Mvangeli was a sympathetic man and was touched by the appeal of Diliza's father. He agreed to take no further steps in the matter, despite the protests of his sons. He refused to accept the self-imposed fine of a sheep, saying it was inadequate compensation for the assault on his daughter. In fact, he added, no payment, either in money or in kind, could ever be adequate compensation for rape or attempted rape. He would try to forget the incident, and hoped that his family would try to forget it too.

IV | *Ntombi*

It was the twilight of dawn, when the morning star alone was shining in the heavens above, and only the horns of the cattle could be seen in the kraal, on the day following Dakada's punishment of Ntombi. Dakada had not slept two hours before he woke up and saw his wife towering above him as he lay stretched on the grass mat. He was uncertain whether he was awake or asleep. He had been dreaming that his wife was denouncing him before a mob of angry people, accusing him of murder, and his daughter was lying near him, covered with a blanket. There was a group of women standing behind his wife, urging their husbands to attack and kill him because he had killed his daughter. The men looked doubtful and unwilling, though they carried stout sticks in their hands, and he himself was unarmed. Suddenly one of the women jumped at him and snatched his blanket away from him, leaving him naked. It was at this point that Dakada woke up and saw his wife standing over him, his blanket tossed to one side. He was lying naked on the mat. His wife spoke.

'Wake up, husband, wake up,' she snapped. 'Wake up. You can't sleep while the child is dying. She hasn't stopped crying and she's as hot as if she has just escaped from hell.

You can't sleep in comfort here while my child is sick with pain from your assault. Get up and do something.'

'What do you expect me to do?' asked Dakada, annoyed at being disturbed so rudely.

'You must go for a doctor at once,' she hissed.

Dakada sat on his haunches, reached for a blanket and wrapped it round his body. His dream had chastened him a little. It had given him a vague sense of having been wrong, of having been too harsh in his punishment. But he still had enough wits about him not to betray this feeling of guilt. He believed that if you give your woman even half a chance, she will 'ride you without a saddle' as horsemen say when stressing the ease with which a tame horse is managed. So he blustered.

'No doctor will wake up at this time and come all the way here to attend to her.' He reached for his pipe, filled it with tobacco from his goat-skin pouch, lit it and began to puff quietly. But his wife kept up a volley of taunts which were only a degree less than insults.

'The black doctor will come if you tell him it's a serious case. You are too lazy to go, that's your trouble. After assaulting my child, you refuse to go for a doctor. After taking sides against her, and defending that filthy slut, you are unwilling to help her in her suffering.'

'Are you quite certain the girl needs a doctor?' asked Dakada.

'Of course I'm certain! What a question to ask! If you were not such a murderous brute, you also would have known that your assault was violent and cruel. Don't squat there like a baboon! Get up and go for a doctor!'

'I'll sjambok you if you've lost your brains,' Dakada growled at her.

'Go on, sjambok me. That's all you know, sjambokking women and children. But remember, I have brothers who will deal with you if you assault me.'

'No brother of yours will bully me in my own house. I deal with my wife and children as I think fit,' answered Dakada.

'If you refuse to go for a doctor,' said Mamtolo suddenly, turning towards the door, 'I shall go to the neighbours and ask for help. I'll find somebody willing to ride to town. Then you can sleep with your mouth wide open while your child is dying.'

After this final thrust Mamtolo went out and banged the door behind her. Dakada decided to follow her to the maidens' hut, where he found Ntombi sobbing quietly, beads of perspiration on her forehead. In his heart Dakada was convinced that it was the evil spirit inside her that made the girl sweat and cry for so long, but he did not say so to his wife. And he was not far from the truth. It was not the punishment which made Ntombi cry. It was her hatred of Zuziwe. It was the thought that her father had sided with the Bhele girl and had assaulted her on that account. She almost choked with anger when she realized that Zuziwe, who could not fight, had used the arm of her father, Dakada, to inflict more pain on her than she, Ntombi, had inflicted on Zuziwe. She thought of several ways of retaliation and rejected all of them because the men would hinder her.

Dakada stood looking at Ntombi for a while. Then he called out loud, 'Ntombi!'

There was no reply.

'Ntombi! What's the matter?' he asked in a louder voice.

There was still no reply, and the sobs became deeper.

'Stop shouting at her,' said Mamtolo. 'That's not the way to cure her. I told you to go for a doctor. I didn't ask you to come and howl at her. You ought to know that your very presence must make her feel worse.'

'All right,' he said. 'I'll wake Zisani up and tell him to go to town and fetch Dr Sango.' Dakada decided to yield to his wife for the sake of his peace of mind.

Zisani went to the cattle-kraal, where the horses were shut in with the cattle. Only two people at Kwazidenge had built stables for their horses. These were Mvangeli Langa and Ntabeni Mlilo. The others either knee-haltered them and let them loose in the veld, or tethered them to a tree with a rope, or kept them with their cattle in the cattle-kraal. Zisani put a halter round the horse's head and led it to the tree under which he had put the bridle and saddle. These he put on the animal and rode off at an ambling walk until he reached the main road, when he urged it into a steady gallop. The horse shied occasionally from dark objects near the road, but Zisani kept his seat and skilfully controlled the horse. When he reached Dr Sango's house, he alighted and tied the bridle-reins to a fence post. He opened the front gate, wondering whether there were dogs in the yard and whether they would allow him to approach the house. He held his riding whip firmly in his right hand to ward off the dogs if they attacked him. Fortunately, he was able to walk right up to the front door and knock unmolested. After he had knocked three times, a light was switched on in one of the rooms and he heard someone inside the house approaching the front door. Mrs Sango opened the door.

'What's wrong, Zisani? Your name is Zisani, is it not?'

'Yes, ma'am, that is my name. I am Zisani Dakada. My sister is very ill at home at Kwazidenge. My father has sent me here for the doctor.'

'The doctor is not in. He's on night duty at Mthwaku Hospital.'

'Do you think he'd come with me if I go to the hospital to ask him?' asked Zisani anxiously.

'I don't know. I doubt it. He's the only doctor on duty tonight. I doubt if he could leave all those patients alone at the hospital and go so far away.'

'But what can I do?' asked Zisani. 'The white doctors will refuse to go to Kwazidenge at this time, even if I can find them.'

'Is your sister very ill? Can't you hire a taxi and take her to the hospital so that Dr Sango may attend to her there?'

'I don't know how bad she is, ma'am. I didn't see her myself. There was nothing wrong with her last night. It must be something sudden. But she must be very ill, otherwise my father would not have asked me to come for the doctor.'

'I don't think the doctor can come to your home earlier than four tomorrow afternoon – or rather this afternoon as it's already morning now. I suggest that you take your sister by car to the hospital at once or bring her here at twelve noon. I'll tell the doctor about her and he'll attend to her first. There's nothing more I can do.'

Zisani had to accept this advice. He rode back home and explained the position to his father. Mrs Dakada urged her husband to hire a taxi to take Ntombi to the hospital. Dakada was unwilling to spend money on a taxi for one who, he was convinced, was not really ill. His wife insisted and he had to go and find a taxi. When Ntombi arrived at the hospital, accompanied by her mother, Dr Sango had already gone off duty. A white doctor examined Ntombi. He was shocked when he saw the sjambok cuts all over her body. He would report the matter to the police, he said, and he urged Mrs Dakada to come forward and speak up against her husband. But Mrs Dakada refused to have anything to do with the police.

'If you dare set the police on my husband,' she warned the doctor, 'I shall stand up and fight you.'

'Do you want your husband to murder your daughter? He'll kill her next time if he's not checked.'

'No. I don't want anybody to hurt my daughter. But I don't want to be helped by the police to restrain him. And what can the police do anyway? He'll probably be fined or imprisoned. And what good will that do us? The money which would have been used to buy food and clothes for me and my children will be paid to the courts. The magistrate will not give us a cent of that money. We'll be left ragged and starving. Keep the police and the law courts out of this, doctor. My family can deal with it.'

'This type of conduct must be discousraged,' protested the doctor. 'This is a very bad example to other husbands.'

'What have I to do with other husbands? Their wives can set the police on them if they choose to do so. I shall fight you if you try to arrest the father of my children, I promise you that. If you wish to arrest somebody, go and arrest Zuziwe Langa, who started all the trouble.'

When the doctor asked about Zuziwe and what she had to do with the affair, he was told about the fight between Ntombi and Zuziwe and its consequences. He realized that the case was too complicated for him and gave it up. He gave Ntombi treatment: first he had her X-rayed, then he gave her an ointment to apply to the cuts. Ntombi was not really ill, he assured them, after he had read the X-ray report. The X-ray revealed no internal damage, and she would be up and about before the day was over. The ointment would help reduce the pain and the cuts would not take long to heal.

The suggestion which Mrs Dakada had lightly thrown at the doctor, that Zuziwe should be arrested, set Ntombi thinking. Zuziwe's arrest would give her much satisfaction, if it could be contrived. And why not? Such things had been done at East London where she had lived before she was endorsed out under the influx control laws. It was easy to get the victim arrested instead of the assailant. It only required a little cunning and quick action. If you went to the police first and made up a good story, the victim became the defendant and the assailant the complainant.

'Mama,' said Ntombi, while they were waiting at the hospital, 'please ask the taximan to take us to the police station at Qoboqobo on our way home.'

'What for, my child?' asked her mother.

'To ask the police to arrest Zuziwe. I have decided to lay a charge against her for assaulting me at Xesi river. I can get

Nomi and the other girls to witness that she assaulted me. She has no witnesses.'

'It's dangerous to do that, Ntombi, my child. Police offices and courts of law are not places for doing a mbhayizelo dance.'

'There's no danger at all, mama. If you complain first to the police, you are quite safe. I have given evidence many times at the Magistrates' Courts at East London and I know them well. A court case is like a railway steam-engine. If it's facing one way, it's not easy to make it turn round and face the other way. If I am the complainant and Zuziwe the defendant, it won't be easy to turn the case round. So we will be quite safe.'

'I understand, but I don't like it. If you grab a snake and set it on an enemy to make it bite him, it might turn round and bite you. I want to have as little to do with the police as with snakes. But I shall do as you ask. There's a sergeant at Qoboqobo Charge Office who is related to us. If he's on duty, he'll give us good advice.'

The taxi came and took Ntombi and her mother to the Charge Office. A statement was taken from Ntombi after she had lodged a formal complaint against Zuziwe. On the following day two policemen drove out to Kwazidenge in a police van and took statements from Ntombi's three friends, Nomi, Makaziwe and Nompongo. From Nompongo's home the van moved slowly on the uneven road and stopped in front of Mvangeli's house. The people of Kwazidenge village came out of their houses to watch. Those who were daring enough went nearer to have a closer look.

The police were polite. They explained to the old man that a complaint against Zuziwe had been made at the Charge Office, and they had orders to take her to Qoboqobo for questioning. She was not under arrest. The senior officers would decide what to do after she had made a statement and further investigations had been made. Mvangeli could accompany his daughter if he wished. The constables refused to give Mvangeli details of the complaint except to say that Ntombi Dakada was the complainant. When Mvangeli protested and told them that they were arresting the wrong person, that they should arrest Ntombi, who had assaulted his daughter, the constables replied that they were carrying out instructions, and that Mvangeli would be given the opportunity to speak up at the Charge Office.

Mrs Langa went wild with anger against Ntombi, against Ntombi's mother whom she accused of witchcraft, against the police, against injustice. The two constables were patient. They paid no attention to her angry words. Mvangeli tried to calm her, and to soothe and reassure Zuziwe, who was sobbing quietly into her handkerchief as she followed her father into the police van. The neighbours came afterwards to the home of the Langas to comfort Mrs Langa as if there was a death in the family. When they advised her to consult a powerful sanuse, as this was a clear case of witchcraft, she told them that Mvangeli would refuse to do that. She herself was inclined to think as they did, but Mvangeli would rather die than have dealings with a sanuse.

After Zuziwe had given a detailed statement to the investigating officer, and after Mvangeli had described all that had happened at Dakada's home, and the punishment given to Ntombi by Dakada, he was allowed to return home with Zuziwe, pending further investigations by the police. After three days a police constable went to Mvangeli's home to tell Zuziwe that the case against her had been withdrawn. Ntombi and her three friends had held on to their story despite detailed questions and threats by the sergeant in charge of the case. All four girls told the same story almost word for word. The two little Thembu girls who had seen Ntombi assault Zuziwe were useless as witnesses. They contradicted each other on several points.

It was Dakada who had compelled Ntombi to withdraw the case by threatening to turn her out with her mother if she refused to do so. Mvangeli gave a sigh of relief. He felt thankful that he himself had relented towards Diliza Mququ's father and had not gone to the headman to lodge a complaint against Diliza. The strain on him, on Zuziwe, and on Zuziwe's mother too, would have been unbearable if they had taken legal action against Diliza. Zuziwe felt grateful to Dakada. He was indeed like the good giant who rescued helpless people from the toils of the evil monsters of folk tales.

V | *Ntabeni at Church*

Ntabeni Mlilo had arranged to meet Zuziwe after the afternoon service on Sunday. He had been told of the fight between Zuziwe and Ntombi and its cause. So, he was keen to meet Zuziwe and talk about it. Ntabeni lived with his old mother and a younger sister, Zanele, who had been widowed two years after getting married. Zanele's husband had been killed in a rockfall in a gold mine near Johannesburg. There were also two little girls and a boy, children of Ntabeni's cousins, living with them. The Mlilos were church people. Zanele's husband had been a keen member of the young men's church guild. Ntabeni, who was twenty years older than Zuziwe, was a lay preacher and deacon of the Presbyterian Church of Africa. But he had two notable weaknesses, an unquenchable thirst for home-made beer and a short temper. He was often found at beer-brewing homes when he should have been attending a deacons' meeting. One of the duties assigned to him by the priest and elders was to collect the monthly contributions of ten cents from each full member of the church. He went on his rounds on Saturdays when his week's work on his plot of land was done. He did not limit his visits to the homes of church members, but he called quite frequently at the homes of other villagers too. During seasons of plenty he collected more beer into his stomach than church contributions into the money bag.

On this particular Sunday, the Sunday after the fight, Ntabeni got up at seven o'clock in the morning and went to the cattle-kraal to milk the cows. He was assisted by his nephew, who brought the milk pail which contained a little water with which to wash his hands. Then the boy tied the cow's hind legs together with a leather strap. Ntabeni sat on his haunches under the cow, pushed the calf away, moistened the cow's udder with a bit of water, and then milked the cow. When he stopped milking, the pail was full to the brim. There was always plenty of milk in Ntabeni's house. He was indeed a prosperous peasant, a fortunate man, by Kwazidenge standards. He possessed the material things of this world in abundance. He was the owner of a large herd of cattle of which he was proud. It gave him an important status in the community. He doubted if he would have won Zuziwe if it had not been for his status as a thriving peasant and owner of a respectable herd. It was this herd which would finally bring the young bride to him. He had already selected the cattle that would be sent to the Langa home. He looked forward with keen anticipation to the day when Zuziwe would be brought. But his herd would be considerably reduced and he was not happy about that aspect: hence his delay in paying the balance of eight head of cattle to make the twelve demanded by the Langa family.

Ntabeni shaved himself clean and smooth when he returned to his hut. The two little girls brought in a large iron bath containing warm water. For fifteen minutes he enjoyed giving himself a thorough wash. During the week he usually limited his ablutions to his hands, face, armpits and feet, using an enamel washbasin. But on Sunday mornings he gave every part of his body a thorough scrub. When he emerged from the bath, he felt good and clean, with the week's accumulation of dirt all left behind in the water. He called loudly to his little nieces and they came and took his bathful of dirt and threw it away. The earth exposed her son's filth to the alchemy of the sun and the wind and the rain and in time transmuted it into a mixture of grass and weeds.

Coffee was brought to Ntabeni by his sister, Zanele, who sat and chatted with him for a while. It was Zanele who had brought Ntabeni the unpleasant report about the Ntombi–Zuziwe fight. Zanele's informant had been a close companion of hers, who had been given what had been described as a reliable report by another member of their circle of friends. Zanele had visited Ntombi to satisfy her curiosity about the details. Ntombi had given her a full and accurate account of the actual fight and the events which followed it. But both Zanele and Ntabeni could not say whether Zuziwe was guilty or innocent of the charge laid against her by Ntombi. It was for this reason that Ntabeni had sent a note to Zuziwe fixing an appointment for Sunday afternoon. Zuziwe had agreed to the appointment.

Ntabeni was a tall, hefty, mountain of a man, a hard-working, thriving peasant who was in his element whenever he was working on the soil. He tilled his plot of ground with great care. He went to bed early in the evening and woke early in the morning, a routine which ensured him success as a farmer. He worked hard the whole day, especially during the ploughing and reaping seasons. He slept well when he went to bed. He had a great capacity for enjoying himself on days when he did not work in the fields, especially on Saturdays and on those days when there was a wedding or a funeral. Despite the fact that he worked hard, however, he had grown flabby. He was as clumsy as a clod, and he looked older than he really was. He dressed himself with great care, in a tight-fitting brown suit on Sundays and at weddings, and in a black suit at funerals. His brown suit had fitted him well when he bought it some four or five years ago, but now it had shrunk and he had expanded.

A dish of sheep's tripe and bread swimming in watery gravy was brought in by Zanele and Ntabeni feasted like a hungry bedbug. He ate all the tripe and bread and drank the gravy with relish. He sucked it from the dish into his mouth like a suction-pump and drained it to the last drop. A mug full of thick sour milk was placed before him, and he drank it all. He concluded the feast with ripe, golden tolofiya fruit. It was a wonder to see all the food disappear into the stomach of one normal person without producing any ill effects.

When it was time for Ntabeni to go to the afternoon service, he took his bamboo-cane walking stick which was curved at the handle end and shod with a small, tight-fitting iron cup at the other end. He packed his Bible and hymn book into a small suitcase and walked slowly to church. The church was on a rising knoll in the sinquma section of the village. On the way he met many people with whom he exchanged greetings and observations on their state of health, and the general health of the village. The first bell was ringing as he slowly approached the church. A boy had been sent by the elder-in-charge to ring the bell. Ting-ting! Ting! Ting-ting! The bell rang for several minutes, sometimes slowly and hesitantly, sometimes joyfully and confidently, according to the mood of the bell-ringer. It called the villagers to the church which gave the sinner the opportunity to go and cleanse his soul of the sins that had accumulated during the week, just as on Sunday mornings Ntabeni washed his body clean of the week's filth. It called to the villagers in every home, men and women, converts and non-converts, to go to the church on the hill as the blowing horn often called to all warriors to assemble on the Hill of Fools for a faction fight. Some responded promptly, others slowly. Some did not respond at all. They tried to ignore it. They pretended there was no bell ringing, demanding their attention. Ting-ting! Ting-ting-ting! Ting-ting! The piercing sound of the bell pricked their consciences and made them feel uneasy in their skins as they sat drinking their beer or exchanging gossip on the people of the village.

Ntabeni was one of the few villagers who responded promptly to the bell. It was not faith alone which produced his prompt response. He was a human being with human motives. He was a deacon with authority, inside and outside the walls of the church, and with important duties to perform. The church gave him a feeling of importance which he enjoyed in no other sphere of village life. In addition to the collection of church tithes, it was his duty to visit and pray for the sick and the bereaved, and to bring the attention of the higher officials of the church to those members who were in adversity. He enjoyed the feeling of importance he experienced during church services. He exercised his authority with firmness and ostentation. He ushered people to their seats, moving some from the back rows to the front with quiet insistence. He consulted the elder-in-charge quite frequently. This whispered consultation gave him the greatest delight, especially when he adopted his favourite pose, his ear turned to the elder so that the latter might whisper into it, his eyes fixed intently on the opposite wall as if he saw nothing, whereas he was really watching the faces of the women and noting the impression he made on them. He loved to give his responses loudly and clearly whenever a person he favoured was praying. He sang in a high, unrestrained tenor voice which was heard by everyone inside and outside the church building. Those who were so unfortunate as to be near him did not have a comfortable time during the service.

When Ntabeni reached the church building, he found the elder sitting under a tree, reading his Bible. After they had shaken hands and exchanged detailed accounts of each other's health and the health of their families and their acquaintances, Ntabeni went inside to see that everything was ready for the service. He opened all the windows, put the seats straight, inspected the collection plates and put them within easy reach, picked up a few pieces of paper and threw them away. Satisfied that all was in order, he went outside and chatted with the people who had already arrived.

As the preacher had not yet come, and it was time for the service to begin, Ntabeni consulted the elder, who instructed him to ring the second bell. If the preacher failed to come, he, the elder, would conduct the service himself. Ntabeni rang the bell and the people went in and took their seats. The first hymn was sung and a prayer followed. Then the Lord's prayer was sung. The second hymn was sung by the choir and the elder read a passage from the Bible. A second elder, who had arrived a few minutes after the service began, was called upon to make the announcements. He urged the members to pay their church dues promptly. He appealed to the deacons to go regularly on their rounds. Reports had been made to the church session that some deacons neglected their work. They allowed their official visits to degenerate into social calls and conducted themselves in a manner that was unworthy of church leaders. When the elder said this, many people turned round and looked at Ntabeni, who flushed with guilt and looked angrily at the elder. Other people, especially the bigger girls, looked at Zuziwe, who had arrived late and had been shown to a seat by Ntabeni. She looked intently at the elder but showed neither anger nor embarrassment. After the announcements, a hymn was sung. This was followed by the sermon:

'The words to which the Lord has pointed for today's sermon are found in Psalms, Chapter 136, Verse 1. Chapter 136 of the Psalms of David, Verse 1. "O give thanks unto the Lord for he is good: for his mercy endureth for ever."'

The preacher read the text a second time, and a third time.

'I wish to apologize to this holy congregation for the preacher who has not come. You will starve today because I have not prepared to preach to you. But all is in the hands of God. In His wisdom He has chosen me to expound the glad tidings to you this afternoon. I know that He will make the right words come from my mouth. In this chapter, David reminds us of the great wonders that God in His mercy has done. Not only did He create the universe, the earth and the sea, the great lights, the sun to rule by day, the moon and the stars to rule by night, but He showed His mercy to His chosen people when He killed the first born of Egypt and destroyed Pharaoh's hosts in the Red Sea, when He smote and slew great and famous kings and gave their land to the Israelites for a heritage.'

And so the preacher preached on, with blazing eyes and clenched fists. He praised the military God who took sides in human conflicts, who showed His great mercy and infinite love by wholesale destruction of the Egyptian hosts, by merciless slaughter of innocent children, and by slaying famous kings and robbing them of their lands. He warmed up to his sermon. He felt that divine inspiration had come. The people caught his inspiration and gave frequent responses. Some of the women sniffled and the men groaned. The younger children were frightened when one of the women, a notorious gossip, became so agitated by her sins that she burst out into loud, hysterical cries. Ntabeni led the congregation in singing a hymn to cover the disturbance. The preacher, encouraged by this response to his sermon, grew more eloquent. He punctuated the hymn-singing with stirring calls to the people to come forward and surrender themselves to Christ, to confess their sins as David did, to acknowledge God as their ruler and king. Three women and a man came forward and knelt on a bench in front of the pulpit to signify that they were offering themselves to Christ.

The preacher decided to end his sermon at this dramatic point. He called on one sister and one brother to pray. One of the elderly women prayed. When she stopped, Ntabeni took his chance. He had been praying for this opportunity. He wished to attack the elder who had made the announcements. He burst out even before the hymn-singing, after the woman's prayer, had ended. He prayed in a loud voice, the loudest he could produce, pitched at a high note so that it could be heard above the singing and silence any other man who might have intended to pray. He prayed eloquently. He had a wide selection of ready-made phrases and quotations. They had obviously been tried out and thoroughly rehearsed on several occasions of public praying. Sometimes he prayed as if a praise-poet was speaking praises to a great chief at an important ceremony. At other times his appeal was more personal. It touched on his own transgressions. He prayed as if he held God by the hand and was speaking to Him face to face. There were two motives behind his prayer. First, he wished to punish the elder who had offended him. Then he wished to impress Zuziwe. He wanted her to feel how foolish she was if she really preferred a Thembu boy to him. He did not mind impressing the other women too. But he could not bear the thought of the woman to whom he had promised marriage showing a preference for another man. The very thought of losing Zuziwe made him feel hot all over his body. He was determined, therefore, to pray in such a way that the foolish girl would see her folly and banish all thought of the hated stranger.

These were the thoughts primarily in Ntabeni's mind. Now he was concentrating on the prayer, calling forth all the phrases which never failed to stir the hearts of human listeners, if not the heart of God. He prayed:

'Have mercy on us, O thou Lion of Judah! Great bull that reigns over all things on earth, in the seas, in the skies, right up to the third heaven above! Swallow that flies among the clouds! Thou wert. Thou art. Thou shalt be to the very end of the universe. Save us, O Lord, from the wiles of the devil and all the other demons under him. Save us from the burning fire of hell. Help us to prepare for our last days on earth when the blue fly buzzes round us as we lie helpless on the mat of death.

'Open our hearts, O God, to the great words spoken by Thy servant today. Teach us to love our neighbour as Thy son loved us. Change the hearts of those elders of this church who sow confusion in the minds of Thy people, who tell lies and slander innocent people. God, their hearts are black with evil and their hands are soiled with dirt. Purify their hearts with a whiff of Thy holy spirit and wash their bodies with holy water, lest they be damned for ever.'

The prayer was received with deep sighs and groans by the congregation. Some women nudged each other. Others opened their eyes and looked at one another and giggled. Zuziwe sat quiet as if she heard nothing. The elder who was the target of this attack kept a dignified silence. He merely remarked after the service that church people were wallowing in mud and that the church would have to work hard to wash them clean.

After Ntabeni had shut all the windows and locked the

doors of the church, he followed the path which Zuziwe had taken, the path which led to her home on the Slope. She was walking alone, slowly, and Ntabeni soon overtook her.

'Did you enjoy today's service, Zuziwe?' asked Ntabeni, after the usual preliminaries.

'Yes, bhuti, I enjoyed some of it.'

'Which part?'

'I liked the sermon and the singing.'

'What did you think of that rogue, the elder who tried to ridicule me? I don't think he'll do that again, the dirty pig. I hit him hard in my prayer.'

'That's the part I didn't like. I think the whole thing was unworthy of Christians.'

'Surely you don't blame me, sithandwa. The man attacked me and I had to hit back,' said Ntabeni, confident of winning the sympathy of Zuziwe. But the words used made her wince. They reminded her of Ntombi's unprovoked assault and of the old hostility between the Thembus and the Hlubis.

'The whole thing was bad, bad at any place, at any time,' she replied. 'But it was worse at church, after a sermon which taught us to be thankful for God's goodness and mercy. I am not taking sides. Both of you were wrong. The elder should have criticized you before a committee such as the Deacon's Court, not at church, certainly not in the presence of the whole congregation.'

'Yes, yes, you agree with me, after all. It's clear even to a girl that he was wrong.' Ntabeni said this with a feeling of triumph, happy that the person who was most important to him was on his side.

'But you too were wrong, bhut' Ntabeni,' Zuziwe hastened to add. 'You were very wrong. You were guilty of blasphemy, almost. A prayer should be humble, not angry. You should ask for forgiveness of sins, in humility, when you pray. You should not feel arrogant and righteous, nor should you feel that the man you don't like must be wrong.'

'But Zuziwe, if you love me, you must side with me in this matter. You must accept my judgement not only because I am a man and I am older than you, but because I am a church official who knows and understands these things better than you.'

'You can be wrong in spite of all that,' Zuziwe insisted, looking straight into his eyes.

Ntabeni was annoyed. He felt that his position as a man, as the dominant partner in their love relationship, was being challenged. He decided to assert himself.

'I forbid you to speak further on this,' he said, forgetting that he had introduced the subject. 'I didn't arrange this appointment for us to quarrel over church matters. I want you to tell me all about your fight with Ntombi.'

'But I told sis' Zanele everything and she promised to tell you all I told her.'

'Yes, yes, Zanele told me all she knew. But there are some things that I want you to clear up.'

'What things?'

'Is it true that you were alone at the river with that boy, Bhuqa, when Ntombi and the other girls arrived?'

'We were not alone. There were many Thembu boys and girls swimming in the river.'

'But the swimming pool is far from the stone on which

you sat,' said Ntabeni, trying not very successfully to control his temper.

'It is,' replied Zuziwe quietly.

'You admit then that you sat alone with that boy. How long did you sit with him?'

'I don't know. It wasn't very long. But why do you ask me all this, bhuti?'

'How could you behave in such a disgraceful manner, Zuziwe? Why did you sit with a boy, a strange boy from a hostile village? Why did you do it, Zuziwe? It's disgraceful that a girl who is engaged to be married to me should sit alone with a boy at the river.'

'Is a girl who is engaged to be married not allowed to speak with a boy? Did you expect me to run away when the boy came and spoke to me?'

'Don't try to be clever with me, I warn you, Zuziwe. I don't wish to be rough on you. But you must not try to be too smart. You know very well you could have sent the boy away from you, or you could have filled your bucket with water and gone away from the river.'

'Yes, I could have done that. But if he had walked with me, he would have been attacked by our boys and people would still have blamed me for luring him into danger. He sat with me quietly and went away peacefully. He was more decent and respectful than some of our own Hlubi boys. It's those girls who caused all the trouble. Don't blame me for it. Blame your own cousin.'

'Do you dare tell me to my face that you were more interested in the safety of that boy than in your good name and my good name? Ntombi was quite right to hit you. I feel like doing it myself. You are a loose, filthy thing, young as you are. I don't want a girl who is the playground of every man in the village.'

'If that is how you feel about me,' replied Zuziwe angrily, 'I feel the same about you. I didn't make love to you. You came to me and asked me to marry you. If you wish to break our engagement, it suits me very well. The sooner the better.'

The words were hardly out of Zuziwe's mouth when Ntabeni attacked her with his walking stick. He hit her hard on her thighs, arms, shoulders and bottom. Zuziwe tried to run away, but Ntabeni, for all his weight, was able to pin her down and she could not escape from him. He stopped only when she sent out piercing cries. Then he said, panting:

'That'll teach you not to trifle with me. I promised to marry you. You accepted me. Your parents gave their consent. I certainly mean to go through with it. I don't want any nonsense from you.'

Zuziwe did not speak. She sobbed into her handkerchief and walked slowly on to her home. Ntabeni walked beside her for some time, but as Zuziwe gave no reply to further questions from him, he left her alone and went back to his home.

VI | *Zuziwe and Bhuqa*

Two weeks after Ntabeni had assaulted her, Zuziwe decided to visit her malume who lived in the Thembu village. She left home early on a Saturday morning. She crossed the Xesi river at the ford where she had met Bhuqa and fought Ntombi. There was nobody at the river as she crossed. The children who came to swim, the young women who came to fetch water, the boys who came to idle, usually came at midday or in the afternoon. The noise made by the rushing water was not exactly frightening, but it inspired Zuziwe with awe. The volume of water was larger than usual because rain had fallen the previous day. The water had taken the brown colour of mud. The stepping stones would help her to cross the river safely. Most of the stones showed clearly above the water, but there was one which was almost submerged. Zuziwe took off her shoes and carried them in her hands. Bare feet gripped stones more firmly than shoes. She crossed confidently until she came to the stone that was partially submerged. She hesitated. She hoped the stone was not slippery and her feet would hold firm. She debated whether she should jump onto the stone and stop, or whether she should jump and pass on to the next stone with the same momentum. She decided that it was safer to jump and stop to regain her balance. She was just about to jump when she was stopped by a voice from the bank in front of her, a voice which made her heart beat faster. It was Bhuqa. She always reacted to his voice as if a current had passed into her body, which opened up at once, ready to absorb the pleasant flow of his love.

'Wait, Zuziwe, wait. Let me come and help you.'

Bhuqa ran towards Zuziwe, hopping nimbly from stone to stone. He stepped on the half-submerged stone and held out his hand to Zuziwe, who jumped onto the stone with confidence. But the stone was too narrow for two people. Bhuqa lost his balance and they fell into the water. He held Zuziwe firmly in the strong current. They waded in the water which reached up to their thighs and held on to large boulders and projecting ledges. Bhuqa kept his balance and supported Zuziwe. He knew that they would be swept away by the current if he slipped, and that Zuziwe, though a good swimmer in calm waters, would be helpless in the dangerous current. She would be tossed about and hurled against the sharp stones. He alone could save her now. They made their way slowly, painfully, through the current. Zuziwe fell once, but Bhuqa kept his foothold and helped her to regain her balance. They went through the dangerous part of the river and crossed over to the Thembu side. Their clothes were soaked and they had to walk to the Thembu village in wet garments. But they were happy to be together, especially after their narrow escape from danger.

'Oh Bhuqa,' said Zuziwe, a light shining from her eyes, 'I was so frightened. But when you held me, I lost all my fear, even when we fell into the current. I think danger itself must be afraid of you and fears to touch me when you are near.'

'Don't talk nonsense,' laughed Bhuqa, gleaming with pleasure. 'Tell me, where are you off to so early?'

'To your village, to visit my malume.'

'That's very good news. When will you visit us? Does Notizi know you are coming? How long will you stay with your malume?'

'Which of these questions am I expected to answer?' she asked, smiling and amused at Bhuqa's excitement.

'All of them. And make them good answers.'

'Do you want good answers or true answers?'

'Both. If they are good answers, they must be true answers.'

'Is that so? I suppose a good answer is an answer that pleases you.'

'Of course. But you haven't answered my questions yet. Do you want me to forget them?'

'No, why should I? I don't know when I shall visit your home. Notizi doesn't know I'm visiting my malume, but please tell her to come and see me today. I have about one week to stay. Do these answers satisfy you?'

'Yes, they are good answers and they do satisfy me. There was an important question, a very important question, which I asked you last time. You wanted time to think. You've had plenty of time. I hope you are ready with your answer now? I want a good, satisfactory answer.'

'What question is this? Please remind me. I think I've forgotten it.'

'How could you forget, Zuziwe? Was it not important

to you? I've been thinking about it all the time, hoping that your answer will be what I desire most, and that you will accept the love I offer you.'

'I told you it would take time for me to think over the question. It's only three weeks since I promised to think over it.'

'Why must you take so long? Don't you know what your heart tells you? Can't you answer me now, Zuziwe?'

'I'm engaged to be married to a man. You are only a boy. Where do you get the courage to interfere with a man's fiancée?' asked Zuziwe, a smile playing on her lips.

'If you mean Ntabeni, he doesn't worry me. He's too old for you, while I'm your age. Besides, you must remember that he too was a boy once, and I also shall be a man one day.'

The two lovers, for that was what they really were, walked slowly along the path leading to the Thembu village. The ground sloped sharply near the river, and their path was steep, narrow and stony. Bhuqa plucked berries from a wild siphingo tree near the path and they sat on a stone to eat the fruit. They forgot their wet clothes and grew more and more tender. When Zuziwe opened her mouth to eat one of the berries in her hand, Bhuqa quickly put into the half-open mouth a berry from his own hand. Zuziwe laughingly put her berry into Bhuqa's mouth. Bhuqa felt that he had never before tasted so sweet a berry. The distance from the river ford to the Thembu village was about two miles, but it took Zuziwe and her lover the greater part of the morning to cover it.

They parted before they came within sight of the village.

Bhuqa went back to join a group of Thembu boys whom they had passed sitting under a large mnquma tree, their favourite rendezvous. He went to them with a light heart and a song in his soul. His offer of love had not yet been accepted by the Hlubi girl, but he was almost certain that she loved him and that she would accept him when they met again. The other boys teased him when he joined them. He was still several yards away when one boy spoke to him.

'Hi! Bhuqa!' he called out. 'Has that beauty crowned you today, or is she still kicking you?'

'No, ntanga, she hasn't crowned me yet. But everything tells me she will. When we meet next time, I'm quite sure she'll be mine.'

'What makes you so sure, Bhuqa? How can you know what a girl intends to do? When you think she has fallen for you, you may be shocked by her refusal. And when she appears reluctant and scornful, that's just when she's going to crown you.'

'*Suk' apha!* Away with you!' replied Bhuqa. 'I'm quite sure of myself. Take it from me, when I meet that girl tomorrow or the day after, I shall have something to tell you. I have plenty of experience with girls. I always know when the ground is sloping downwards. I'm running on easy ground now and I shall soon get there.'

'How long is she staying here?'

'About a week, she said. But I can make her stay two weeks or even three.'

'What will you do with your other girls during her stay here? Can I keep one of them for you? I'm sure you'll be so busy enjoying this new one that you will have no time for the others.'

'I don't need your help. I can serve all of them. I warn you or any other boy here to keep away from my girls.'

'I say, Bhuqa,' said another boy. 'I hear this Hlubi girl you are so mad after is engaged to be married to a man at her village. Is this true?'

'Yes, it's true,' replied Bhuqa. 'A man called Ntabeni wants to marry her.'

'What will happen when her parents and this man find out that she is fooling about with you, an uncircumcised boy with a long foreskin?'

'Don't be silly, kwedini. Don't speak like that to me. She doesn't care a bit for that Ntabeni. She told me the man hit her the week before last and she's going to reject him.'

'Do you think her parents will allow her to do that?'

'I don't know and I don't care,' replied Bhuqa. 'I am determined to enjoy as much of her as I can. What happens at her home is no concern of mine.'

'How will you meet each other when she returns home?'

Bhuqa's face clouded a little when this question was asked. But it cleared again and he replied cheerfully, 'Oh, that's no problem. There are many bushes along the Xesi river to serve your purpose, if you and your girl understand each other, and I always make my girls do what I want.'

'You'll have to be careful, Bhuqa. There'll be many eyes spying on you. Remember that some girls assaulted your girl the other day just for sitting and speaking innocently with you at the river ford? There'll be sharp eyes watching her. Ntabeni's jealous eyes will be watching both of you closely.

And those Hlubi girls will be keen to produce proof that their assault was justified. You should always arrange to have us somewhere nearby when you have an appointment with her. Otherwise your death is in it.'

'Well and good,' replied Bhuqa, with a steely glint in his eye. 'If a man attacks me, he'll get as good as he gives, or better.'

Two days later Bhuqa met Zuziwe by appointment. Zuziwe left her uncle's home in Notizi's company early one afternoon. The two friends were dressed alike, in simple, floral cotton frocks and pink, woollen, tight-fitting blouses which made their breasts stand out like ripe apples. They had silk doeks round their plaited hair. They wore flat, polished, brown shoes. Their legs were full and bare from the ankles up to well beyond the knees, and they were smeared with ointment. The two girls were so attractive that they inflamed not only the young men of the village with desire, but made even middle-aged men steal a glance at the girls' legs, though they pretended to be looking at the distant haze of hills and mountains. The older men could not help wishing that they were young and free so that they might have a fling with the girls. But on this glorious, sunny morning, after a day of soaking rain, the girls belonged to Bhuqa, and to Notizi's partner, who accompanied Bhuqa on this love adventure. The four lovers met and walked together, slowly, each pair holding hands. Their carefree laughter blended with the song of chirruping birds and other woodland choristers.

When they came to a bushy patch in the woodland, a popular mating spot of all young lovers of the Thembu village, the two couples separated. Bhuqa and Zuziwe found a spot where the grass was green and clean. There was a leafy tree under which there was a flat stone. Bhuqa sat on the stone and, taking Zuziwe's two hands in both of his, looked deep into her eyes and said:

'Well, sithandwa, what's your decision?'

'About what?' asked Zuziwe, looking back into his eyes.

'You know. About my love offer to you.'

'Bhuqa, tell me this.' Zuziwe spoke quietly, earnestly, like one about to make an important decision. 'You know that Ntabeni of our village has promised me marriage. In making me this love offer, do you promise to marry me if I reject Ntabeni and accept you?'

'Don't talk of marriage, beautiful one. I am too young to promise marriage to you. I have not even been to the circumcision school yet. But this I can say, I love you more than I have ever loved any girl.'

'What about those girls of yours in your village? Have you not said the same thing to them a thousand times?'

'Yes, I have. I don't wish to tell a lie. I have spoken these words to them before. But that was before I met you and loved you. The words were true then. But now I would not say this to them because it would be a lie.'

'So it is true that you are in love with other girls, that you are a playboy, udlalani, as they say. Why do you deceive me, Bhuqa? Why do you tell me that you love me, that you want me to be yours, if you have other girls? Do you want to go about boasting that I am your latest victim?'

'Please cool down and listen to me. Did you expect to find a normal boy of my age without a girl? That's impossible.

Surely you must see that that is impossible. Remember, you yourself are in love with Ntabeni. Why do you become angry when I confess that I have other girls?'

'How many?'

'Two.'

'Why should you have two? Is one girl at a time not enough for you? Must you have two? And now you want a third.'

'I made love to the second one because the first was away from home for several months. She returned home only last week from her mother's home. Her own relatives had told me she would not return but would live there permanently.'

'You have ready excuses for your unfaithfulness. Before I accept you, I must get the assurance that I am to be your only girl.'

'Yes, sithandwa, I give you that assurance most willingly. But I cannot end things now with them. I can't go to the girls and tell them bluntly that I am rejecting them. A girl does that, but not a boy. I shall simply neglect them and then they themselves will reject me.'

'Do you promise that you will never again have anything to do with those girls?'

'Yes, Zuziwe, I do. Do you accept me as your lover?'

'Yes, Bhuqa, I do.'

Bhuqa took her in his arms and kissed her as she had never been kissed before. Ntabeni's kisses had always been cold and short. Zuziwe had always pushed him back after only a few seconds of contact. Long ago, as a little girl, she had had love-affairs with young boys of her age. But there had been no passion in the pecks they called kisses.

This was her first real kiss and it roused her to an ecstasy and an agony of passion. They fitted into each other perfectly for Bhuqa was only a little taller than Zuziwe. The poor girl moaned and twisted and pressed herself into him as if she wanted her body to merge into his. Bhuqa pressed her tightly. He caressed her cheeks, her neck, her back, and ran his fingers into her plaited hair. He squeezed her hard and kissed her hungrily. They rolled over from side to side on the green grass. He kissed her again and again on the open mouth. She kissed him back and drank him in. She surrendered herself completely to him and they lay stretched on the green grass in complete enjoyment of their love. After a while they relaxed from sheer exhaustion and looked at each other, their eyes shining with the light of love.

After a long time the other pair of lovers returned and they walked home together. The two boys stopped at the fringe of the woodland and the girls went on to the village.

Zuziwe's uncle and aunt were pleased that Notizi was keeping their niece well entertained. They were fond of their niece and felt unhappy when she appeared lonely and quiet. Whenever she was in Notizi's company, she was always bright and cheerful. For this reason they encouraged the two girls to visit each other and keep together as often as possible. So, these were pleasant days for the two girls and their lovers, and they passed far too quickly for their liking. After two weeks Zuziwe returned home. Bhuqa took her as far as the river ford. Before they parted, they arranged to meet three days later at a spot which Bhuqa pointed out under a willow tree near the river, on the Hlubi side of the river.

VII | *Love Potion*

On the day following her return home, Zuziwe told her mother that she felt she did not love Ntabeni at all, and that she could not marry him. She said she had decided to write to him and tell him so. Mrs Langa was not surprised. She had always doubted Zuziwe's love for this man who was so much older than she was. She had not noted any of the usual signs of a teenage girl in love. She rarely wrote to him. When he wrote to her, she invariably sent back a message by Ntabeni's own messenger, either verbally or in a short note. After Ntombi's river assault on Zuziwe, and Ntabeni's Sunday afternoon assault, Mrs Langa had become more convinced than ever that Zuziwe would not marry Ntabeni. So she was not surprised when her daughter told her her decision.

'Your father must be told of this before you write to Ntabeni,' she said. 'Your father has already given his consent to Ntabeni's people. He must be consulted before you act.'

'Yes, I know, mama. I hope tata won't try to compel me to marry Ntabeni. My dislike of him grows more and more every day. I would rather die than marry that man.'

'No, Zuziwe, don't say that. You can never know what tomorrow will bring. A person is often compelled by circumstances to do what she doesn't like to do. But you needn't fear your father. He's always gentle and understanding. He won't compel you to act against your wishes in a matter so important for your future happiness, especially if there's another young man, a good young man, who wishes to marry you. Tell me, sana, are you giving up Ntabeni because you have fallen out of love with him or because you have fallen in love with someone else?'

'Both,' replied Zuziwe.

'I thought so. I know my little girl. I noted the radiant look in your face when you arrived yesterday. Your visit has done wonders to you. You are much lighter and much prettier than you were before you left. What has this young man done to my baby? What medicine has he used on you? He has certainly injected new life into you. He is a Thembu, is he not, and lives at your malume's village?'

'Yes, mama, I love him very much. I think I would die if I couldn't have him.'

'What's his name, child? Has he promised to marry you?'

'His name is Bhuqa Ngoma. He says he's still too young to promise to marry me. But he says he loves me more than any other girl he has ever been in love with. He has assured me that he will give up the girl he has been in love with.'

'Is he trying to play tricks? Why does he say he's too young to promise to marry you? Be careful of him, my child. He might disappoint you if you give yourself too eagerly to him. You must hold back something from him. Then he will come out more completely. How old is he?'

'He's two years older than I am. He has not been to the circumcision school yet, mama. He'll go in with the next group of boys.'

Something was nagging at Zuziwe, tormenting her. Towards the end of her stay at the Thembu village, she had felt there was something wrong with her. She did not quite know the symptoms of pregnancy. But she feared she was pregnant. Her period was due in about ten days' time, and then she would know the truth. But now she said nothing.

Her mother did not notice that there was something worrying her daughter. She merely said: 'I hope for your sake, my child, that Bhuqa is reliable. He comes from a good family. I know his parents well. He's the eldest son and will inherit his father's land and cattle. But I wonder what your father and your uncles will say when they are told that you have jilted Ntabeni for a wild, light-headed Thembu boy. They believe that all uncircumcised boys are wild and light-headed. Then there's your brother, Duma. You know how he hates Thembus. You've overturned a stone that's been hiding a large colony of ants, my child.'

'He's not wild, mama, and he's not light-headed. Notizi told me that her father relies very much on him. She told me he's a hard worker. He does most of the work at his home. He always makes it a point to complete his work before he joins the other boys under the mnquma tree at the edge of the forest. He was very bright at school. He passed Standard VI in the first class. He hopes to go to the agricultural school at Fort Cox when he leaves the circumcision school.'

'That sounds well. I hope he really means it. I shall speak to your father as soon as he returns from the fields.'

Mama Langa was confident that her husband would be as reasonable in this as he always was. She knew that he would understand and sympathize with Zuziwe. If he objected, mama Langa was confident that she could persuade him to allow Zuziwe to do as she wished. Mvangeli listened attentively when his wife told him what his daughter had decided to do. He remained quiet for a long time until she became impatient.

'What do you say, father of Zuziwe?' she asked. 'Do you consent?'

'You know very well that I will not compel Zuziwe to marry a man she doesn't want. I know I can compel her to marry Ntabeni, but I don't wish to do that. And yet it's not a thing that may be done lightly, to withdraw consent after it has been given by the family, even though only a few cattle have been paid by the man.'

'The cattle are still in the kraal,' Mrs Langa pointed out. 'They don't matter at all. They don't have to be considered. It would be hard if they had already been used to pay lobola for one of our sons. They are still in the kraal. They can be sent back tomorrow if necessary.'

'Yes, that is true,' said Mvangeli slowly, thoughtfully. 'But still, I have my fears.'

At this point Duma came into the room, the living-room of the cottage. Zuziwe also entered the room from the kitchen. Duma had not yet met Zuziwe since her return from the Thembu village. But he had heard stories of her behaviour during her two weeks' stay there. And Duma was very angry. He did not greet her, nor did he ask her about her health, as was expected after so long an absence. He merely greeted everybody in general as he always did every morning when he came to the main cottage. Zuziwe knew at once that Duma had heard about her love and did not approve. She stiffened and waited, ready to fight for her lover and her baby. She was not yet certain, but she felt that Bhuqa's baby was in her body. That was the way she saw it, a fight for her lover and her baby, the baby in her womb, the baby who had come from Bhuqa's body to her womb, as if by a miracle, in defiance of the hostility in the hearts of the Thembus and the Hlubis. She felt that Duma was as much of a threat to her as Ntombi and her gang. But she would not yield. They might attack her physically and beat her to the ground, but she would not submit. She would resist them until she was either victorious or destroyed.

When Mvangeli told Duma what Zuziwe had decided to do, Duma's anger erupted.

'Zuziwe is talking nonsense,' he fumed. 'She must marry Ntabeni as arranged. I know she's mad for that Thembu boy. I, Duma, will never allow her to marry a Thembu boy, a boy she would hate if she knew what was good for her. Ntabeni must pay the remaining lobola and marry her at once. That's the only way to put a stop to her nonsense.'

'I'll marry Ntabeni only when I am a corpse,' Zuziwe hissed, and with these words she rushed out of the room.

'You are wrong, Duma, very wrong,' said Mvangeli, ignoring Zuziwe's outburst. 'There must be no compulsion in this matter, least of all from you, her eldest brother, her second father, as it were. You have the right to advise Zuziwe, to guide her. But you have no right to compel her to act against her wishes in the choice of her own husband. You are wrong if you think there's an easy solution to this problem. It is bad to break a promise, a solemn promise made on your behalf by your family. But then you must remember that if Zuziwe's life with Ntabeni turns out to be unhappy, she will be the one to suffer, not her brother, not her father, not her relatives. Let there be no compulsion. The final decision must be hers.'

'And you must not forget, Duma,' Mrs Langa added, in support of her husband, 'that there may be peace one day between the Hlubis and the Thembus, and that would mean that my child had given up the man she loves unnecessarily.'

'That Thembu boy will not set foot in this house! If you want to sacrifice your daughter, that's your affair. I can't stop you. Pack her and send her to that Thembu devil and be done with it. But if you allow a Thembu to come here to marry Zuziwe, he dies or I die. Take your choice.'

With these words Duma walked out of the room, stamping hard on the wooden floor. He left behind him an angry mother and a worried father.

'Duma is mad,' said Mrs Langa. 'What does he think he is? Does he think he is the head of this house? You can see how he will treat us when you have passed on, father of Zuziwe. You must not be soft with him. You must teach him his place now, before you die. He must learn to be reasonable like his father. He mustn't threaten us and bully us, and make our life a hell on earth. Let Zuziwe marry the young man she loves, not that bully, Ntabeni, who actually assaults her even before he has made her his wife. Think of it. How will he treat my child when he has a husband's rights over her, if he hits her when he's no more than her fiancé? No wonder Duma favours Ntabeni. They are both of them wild, savage, dangerous bulls. I'll not let my child be sacrificed to a savage so utterly without restraint.'

'Calm yourself, nkosikazi,' said her husband patiently. 'Anger will not solve anything. Don't say things which you will regret afterwards. Both you and Duma are allowing your tempers to master you. Duma threatens to use his stick to solve this problem. He is wrong. Violence does not solve anything. I know he didn't mean what he said. It's his temper which spoke, not the Duma we know. You don't have to take what he said seriously. Besides, I'm not dead yet. I have still many years of life before me. I shall outlive many people much younger than I am. Don't upset yourself over nothing. Let us think over Zuziwe's problem. Let's sleep on it and pray for God's guidance. Perhaps time will bring the right solution.'

On the following day Zuziwe received a note from Ntabeni, fixing an appointment for Sunday afternoon. Zuziwe replied promptly and told him that she had decided to end their engagement and that there could be no appointment for Sunday. Ntabeni was standing at the entrance to the cattle-kraal when the messenger-boy gave him Zuziwe's note. He took it, looked at the address on the envelope, went into his hut and sat on a stool, satisfied at Zuziwe's prompt reply. He opened the note and read it. The smile on his face changed into a frown. He cursed Zuziwe and called her all the filthy things he could think of. Then he grew quieter and looked at the note for a long time, but without seeing it. He stood up and walked about the hut.

'It's that Thembu boy,' he said. 'Ntombi was right. It's that boy who has put all these dirty thoughts into my girl's head. I swear by my ancestors he'll enjoy her in hell. What! Can she prefer a boy, an uncircumcised boy, to me? It's impossible. That boy has bewitched her. But whatever happens he'll not get her. She may give herself to any other lover, but not that Thembu boy.'

Ntabeni took his hat and planted it firmly on his head. Then he took his mthathi stick and came out of his hut. He walked slowly towards Zuziwe's home. He passed several people on the way, some of whom he saw and greeted. But there were many whom he neither saw nor heard as they greeted him. He went straight to the living-room of the Langa cottage and knocked at the door. Mvangeli himself asked him to enter. Mvangeli and his wife were in the room. Ntabeni replied curtly to the older man's enquiry after his health. He plunged straight into the subject which worried him.

'You daughter, bawo Langa, do you know what she has written to me this morning?'

'What has she written?' asked Mvangeli cautiously.

'Don't you know that she has written to me, rejecting me?'

'She told me that she had decided to break off your engagement. I didn't know that she had already written to you about it.'

'Do you mean to say you have allowed her to break off an engagement that has been agreed upon by our families and is known by everybody in the village?'

'She is the best judge in this affair, my son. If she feels she can't go on with the engagement and the marriage, I won't force her. If you can't make it up between the two of you, there's very little that your parents and relatives can do. The other day you used a stick on her. I didn't do anything when it was reported to me. But I felt that you were using the wrong method and that you would not win my daughter's respect and love if you used the language of violence. I was not at all surprised when I was told that she had decided to break off the engagement.'

'Bawo Langa, why don't you act with firmness in this? Surely you have the right to order your daughter to honour her promise? She is childish and foolish and does not know what is good for her. She must submit to you and show respect to my family and yours. If she does not do this, I shall begin to think she has not been properly brought up by her parents.'

'Thole, please, I ask you, let's drop this talk. I'm not going to compel Zuziwe to marry you if she herself doesn't wish to do so. There's no point in discussing the affair.'

Ntabeni left abruptly and went back to his home. He told his mother and his sister, Zanele, that Zuziwe had rejected him. His mother received the information with inward satisfaction. She had not favoured Zuziwe from the first. She was a spoilt child, she thought, and would not make a good wife for her son. Deep down in her subconscious mind there was a streak of jealousy that another woman was threatening to rob her of her only son, a son who had always loved her and her alone. But Zanele burst into a storm of abuse. She felt for her brother. She cursed Zuziwe as Ntabeni had cursed her. Who was she, after all? She was nothing but a cheap, loose whore. How dared she jilt her brother?

She sent a child to go and ask Ntombi to come to her so that they might decide on a plan of action. Ntombi's reaction was a mixture of anger for her cousin's sake and satisfaction that events had proved her right in her accusation and assault of Zuziwe.

'She spent two weeks at her uncle's home at the Thembu village,' observed Ntombi, 'and on her return the first thing she does is to jilt my cousin. There's something between her and that Thembu boy, if you ask me. We must find out what she's up to.'

'I guess they'll try to meet at the river ford or somewhere near there,' said Zanele. 'We must watch her secretly when she goes to the river. We can easily make it impossible for them to meet. Then their affair will die out like a fire of dry twigs.'

'That boy is inviting trouble and he'll get it, I can tell you,' said Ntabeni, in a voice of thunder, and with a scowl as black as a cloud before a hailstorm. 'This has never happened to me before and it will not happen. I will not allow a dog of a boy to take my girl from me. If this boy does not stop, a corpse will come out of this affair, I promise you.'

'You will have to be careful, bhuti,' Zanele warned him. 'I understand that Thembu boy is a great fighter.'

'*Suka!* Away with you!' retorted Ntabeni angrily. 'I don't fear any boy. He'll have to remove his foreskin before he gets the better of me.'

Ntabeni was growing angrier and angrier as he spoke. But his anger was mere bluff. The truth was that he was not a fighter. He knew from experience that it was unwise to tackle a boy single-handed. Boys usually went about in groups. If you tackled one, you might find that his companions were not far off, and you would probably end up with a broken head. And even if the boy was alone, he might fight back. Some boys were not easily intimidated and this Thembu boy, from all reports about him, was probably of this type. Gone were the days when boys did not dare stand up to a man who had been through the circumcision school for fear that all the other men of the village would rise up in violent anger against him. These days everybody minded his own business and tried to keep himself out of other people's troubles. And so Ntabeni fumed and blustered so as to impress the girls, but secretly he resolved that he would be careful in planning any encounter with the Thembu boy.

They took some time discussing ways of upsetting the affair between Bhuqa and Zuziwe. But none of the suggestions gave promise of success.

'I've heard of a man at Jojo village,' said Zanele, finally, 'who is noted for his powerful love potions. My late husband used to tell me that many young Jojo men, and young women too, often used this man's philtres to win the hearts of those who rejected them. I've often felt that he too must have used this man's medicines when he came to make love to me. I loathed him like rotten meat at first, but suddenly one day I felt a gush of love for him and accepted him. I asked him once, after we were married, whether he ever visited this sanuse. He admitted having gone once in the company of a young man who wanted a mixture for himself, although he denied that he himself used these aids to love.'

'Do you know this man's name and where he lives in Jojo village?' asked Ntabeni casually.

'Yes. His name is Gabulamehlo of the clan of Mkwayi. He lives on the outskirts of the village. His home can be seen clearly as you approach Jojo from this side. He is well known there. Any child could show you the place.'

'What you suggest is worth trying, Zanele,' muttered Ntabeni, after moving up and down the hut quietly for a long time. 'Are you certain that his love potions are effective? It would be bad for me, a churchman, to consult a sanuse and risk trouble from the priest and church council, only to fail to make the girl hate that Thembu boy and fall in love with me.'

'He's a famous sanuse, bhuti,' replied Zanele confidently. 'I'm surprised you don't know him. His love potions have never failed, as far as I know. If the girl's mind is strong and unyielding, the philtre has the effect of making her run mad. Soft and yielding natures are safe. To them the philtre is harmless. It just makes the girl fall madly in love with the man consulting the sanuse. I'm sure Zuziwe is of the yielding type. The philtre will not harm her. It would be dangerous for a stubborn person like mzala Ntombi.'

'Don't be silly, mzala. Who would care to use a love potion for a girl as ugly as I am? Marriage is out of the question for me. I am destined to follow my name and remain a girl to the end of my days.'

'You never know, mzala. There are ugly girls who look as if they have been scolded but are happily married and have lovely children. And there are many pretty girls who have made ugly children or have failed to make them at all. I can't understand why a man should choose a pretty girl for a wife. She's just a lot of trouble for her husband, worthless trouble too. Attractive women are unfaithful. Whenever the husband takes a trip and is away from home for a few days, the wife sends at once for one of her former lovers to keep her husband's bed warm for him. I am sure Zuziwe will continue to be the whore that she is even when she's married.'

'What's the use of beauty in marriage anyway?' added Ntombi, pleased at the turn the conversation had taken. 'After a few years of child-bearing and neglect by her husband and disappointment by her lovers, your former beauty queen is no better than the plain-faced woman. It's always the beautiful girls who commit suicide.'

Ntabeni had stopped listening to this denunciation of female beauty. He was thinking hard over Zanele's suggestion, trying to look into the future, to see what possibility of success there was in it, and what repercussions would follow if he used a love potion on a young girl. He knew that villagers, including church officials, were inquisitive gossipers who would soon find out all about his affairs, even if he tried to keep them secret. Would he be excommunicated if Zuziwe became hysterical after taking the love potion, and went up and down raving about him? He knew he could not hope to win her if she turned hysterical. Her parents would not have him after that even if she got well again. Would it not be too much to lose his cherished position in the church and also fail to win the girl? Should he take the gamble on the sanuse or should he play safe? He stopped in front of the girls to discuss the matter further.

'Tell me, Zanele. Mzala Ntombi, tell me. Do you think that boy used a love potion to win the girl? She has given him many chances to do that. She has visited the Thembu village quite often. She's a close friend of the boy's sister. She has been to his home several times. He could have put a love potion into her food. Suppose he has used a philtre to make her crazy over him, do you think mine will be effective?'

'It depends on the strength of the sanuse, bhuti,' replied Zanele. 'Our sanuse is a famous man with strong potions. I don't think Bhuqa could have got his philtre from Gabulamehlo. Jojo village is far from the Thembu village. Besides, the two villages are hostile to each other. I believe even the men and the women of the two villages are not on friendly terms because Jojo boys usually help Hlubi boys when there's a fight between Hlubis and Thembus. If Bhuqa has used a love potion, he must have got it from a smaller man. I tell you Gabulamehlo is the man to go to if you want an effective potion.'

'Mzala Ntombi, do you think Zisani would accompany me to Jojo village tomorrow afternoon? I want to smoke my pipe before it dies out. I must go there at once and I can't go alone. If we went together, I could wait near the Zingcuka river below the village, and Zisani could go to Gabulamehlo for me.'

'Yes, bhut' Ntabeni,' replied Ntombi, 'I think he would, unless he has some special work to do.'

'Bhut' Ntabeni, you yourself must go to the sanuse,' said Zanele. 'The philtre will not work for you if you are not in the room when the sanuse is preparing it. The philtre must see you, as it were, so that it may make the girl see you in her mind and fall in love with you.'

'I know that. Do you think I'm ignorant of these things?

Do you think I know less about this than you do? I was only trying to think of a way of keeping my movements secret. I didn't actually mean I would remain at the river all the time. I shall go to the sanuse if Zisani agrees to accompany me. Makhwenkwe will go along with mzala Ntombi so that he may bring me word today from Zisani.'

Ntombi returned home accompanied by Makhwenkwe, Ntabeni's nephew, who took back the message that Zisani was willing to accompany Ntabeni to the sanuse. And so, on the following day, early in the afternoon, Ntabeni and Zisani set out on foot at a steady pace on their way to Jojo village. The distance was a little under four miles. The road ran along the valley of the Zingcuka river. As they approached Jojo village, the road rose steeply, and the two men slackened their pace. Beyond the village lay the Bhukazana mountain and in the haze beyond lay the Nkonkobe range of mountains. The walk was so strenuous that they were compelled to sit in the cool shade of a large tree beside the Zingcuka river to rest a little before tackling the last steep rise that would take them to their destination. They felt it would not be wise to go into the sanuse's presence wet with perspiration. You had to be cool and collected when making a consultation which would influence the course of your life and the lives of other people. The sanuse must be given a chance to feel the truth and give you the right philtre.

Ntabeni and Zisani were led by Gabulamehlo's assistant into a hut which stood by itself, some distance away from the other huts of the sanuse. Ntabeni did not give this man detailed answers to the questions he asked on behalf of his chief. He doubted the man's integrity. Some of these men have no chest, he explained afterwards to Zisani, and before you know where you are, the details of your visit are known all over, not only in Jojo village, but also at Kwazidenge. So he told Mathambo, the sanuse's assistant, that he was troubled deep inside him. His trouble was so deep, he said evasively, that he himself did not know what it was. He had not come to ask the wise one to *vumisa*, to divine. He himself would speak out, open his insides to the wise one, as it were, so that he might feel his trouble and find a cure for it. Mathambo tried to bully Ntabeni into revealing his thoughts, but Ntabeni refused to be bullied. Mathambo went out reluctantly. He had grown quite curious. The visitors were obviously different from the usual type who consulted the sanuse. It was clear to him that Ntabeni was either a churchman or a school man or both. It was true that there were more of the Ntabeni type who consulted the sanuse than was generally believed. They usually came at night. Mathambo always found these visitors interesting, and their visits were entertaining topics of conversation at beer-parties. Other churchmen who attended the beer-parties were always greedy for gossip about the deviations of their fellow churchmen, while giving strict instructions that their own activities be kept secret.

After fifteen minutes Mathambo returned, followed by the sanuse. Gabulamehlo was a well-built man, a long way away from the ground, as the villagers said when describing his great height. He was sinewy, but not large of limb. He had bright, piercing eyes which made you feel uneasy when he looked at you, as if he could see deep into your soul. You felt you could not conceal the truth from this man.

Mathambo was about to squat at the back of the hut when Gabulamehlo, with an instinct which was perhaps the source of his success as a sanuse, ordered his assistant to leave him alone with the visitors. Mathambo went out very slowly, very reluctantly, but he went out. He could not disobey his chief. His scant bottom appeared scantier than ever in the ample folds of his trousers as he shuffled, barefoot, towards the door and out of the hut. Gabulamehlo went to the door and looked out, to make certain that they were quite alone. He wanted his visitors to feel free to reveal their worries to him. He already knew, from Mathambo's account, that the visitors desired secrecy. One look at Ntabeni when he entered had told him that he had guessed rightly. Ntabeni was obviously a churchman. He was unwilling to reveal his secrets to an assistant. When Gabulamehlo followed Mathambo to the door, and watched him move well away from the hut, it was not because he expected him to eavesdrop. He rather wanted Ntabeni to see that he was taking every precaution to keep his secret so that he might speak more freely. The sanuse knew that the secret of success in medicine lay first and foremost in instilling a feeling of confidence into the patient. If the patient has no confidence in the medicine-man, then the medicine-man labours in vain.

'What is your trouble, my children?' asked the wise one, without preliminaries. 'You know, I am both a sanuse and a medicine-man. From what I learnt from my assistant, you have not come to me to divine, to reveal the truth about you and the future. You want me to prepare you a mixture to help you in some trouble which you rightly refused to reveal to my assistant. Is that right?'

'Yes, wise one. You are right, Gabulamehlo. I'm quite confident that what I reveal will go into you and will be swallowed up as the river water is swallowed up by the great sea. But first you must know who I am. I am Ntabeni Mlilo of isinquma section of Kwazidenge. I am of the clan of Thole, of Ndlangisa, of Mpundeshe, of Mcaca. This is my staff, my mzala, Zisani Dakada of isinga section of our village. He is of the clan of Ndlovu. I didn't have the strength to come alone to see you. He has therefore come so that I may lean on him when the need arises.'

'Yes, my son, it is always wise to rely on your staff when you have an important job to do. Speak on, Ntabeni Mlilo. My ears are open.'

'My story is short but painful. It will not take long to tell. It is a story of love.'

'Love and pain. Those two are inseparable twins, my son. A story of love is always a story of pain, of tears. If there is no pain, if there are no tears, there is no love. But we of our profession make it our business to decrease the pain and tears, and increase the love and happiness. Speak on, Ntabeni Mlilo. I am all ears.'

'I have promised marriage to a sweet, young girl of the Bhele clan down at our village, a girl as bright and beautiful as the clear waters of the Xesi river, and as warm as sunshine in spring. She accepted me, and her family gave their consent to my family, all according to custom, as you know. Suddenly I learnt that a Thembu boy had corrupted my girl when she visited her malume at the Thembu village. Then my girl rejected me. Can you believe it, wise one? My sweet Zuziwe jilted me for a wild, uncircumcised boy. The boy used a love potion, I'm sure of that. Please help me, Gabulamehlo! Give me the strongest philtre in your stock so that I may win back my girl.'

'What makes you certain that the boy has used a love potion? I must be careful, you see. If I give you a strong philtre for a girl who has never taken one before, she will become hysterical or mad.'

'He must have used a love potion, wise one. What other explanation can there be for her rejection of me?'

'How old is this girl? asked Gabulamehlo. 'She must be quite young if she falls in love with an uncircumcised boy. And you are a full-grown man.'

'She's eighteen years of age. She accepted me in spite of the difference in our ages. Age has nothing to do with her rejection of me. *Uphoselwe*, she is bewitched. That's the trouble.'

'Are you willing to take the risk of madness?' asked Gabulamehlo. 'My job is to give satisfaction to the people who appeal to me. If you are willing to take the risk, I can prepare a strong philtre for you, the strongest I have, which I call *Velabahleke*, Appear-and-they-laugh, stronger even than the more popular *Vamna*, Feel-me.'

'I'm willing to take the risk, wise one,' replied Ntabeni.

Gabulamehlo looked at Ntabeni for a while, his bright, clear eyes seeming to penetrate into him and to see his innermost thoughts and feelings. Then he smiled, a smile full of contempt, for he was convinced that this was one of those cases where he could neither increase the love and happiness nor reduce the pain and tears. It was clear that Ntabeni was more in love with himself than with Zuziwe and more concerned with his position and his name in the village than with Zuziwe's well-being. But that was not his business. His was to give satisfaction to the people who came to consult him, not to change the hearts of selfish people. So he made the philtre, explained carefully to Ntabeni how it was to be used, and received twelve rand, the equivalent of two goats, for his services.

Ntabeni's next move was difficult. He had to find an opportunity to make Zuziwe drink the potion. He had to give it to Zuziwe himself, with his own hands. That was the sanuse's instruction: otherwise it would not work. A few drops of the liquid had to be thrown into Zuziwe's food or milk or tea or any other liquid food which would prevent her from detecting the taste of the potion. It would not be possible to invite her to his home. He could not send her a parcel of food or tolofiya fruit or some other wild fruit. He had never done this even when they were engaged. It would be strange to do it now when they had parted. People would be suspicious, and Zuziwe would not eat the food.

Ntabeni, Zanele and Ntombi met quite often but were unable to solve the problem. Zanele offered to serve the potion on Zuziwe with her own hands, hoping it would still work this way. She could visit Zuziwe on the pretext of trying to mend things between her and Ntabeni, and she could easily throw a few drops of the potion into the tea she would be certain to make for both of them. But Ntabeni angrily rejected the suggestion. The instructions were quite clear. He, Ntabeni, must serve the potion himself. His hand must be the last hand to touch the bottle before the potion was poured into Zuziwe's food. If it was Zanele who served the potion, Zuziwe would not fall in love with him.

Ntabeni walked daily up and down the path between the Xesi ford and Kwazidenge village, hoping to meet Zuziwe and offer her a doctored tolofiya fruit he carried in a small tin. His plan was to invite her to sit on the roadside with him for a while and eat the tolofiya fruit just for old time's sake. Zuziwe did not come, except once when she was returning from the river with two of her sisters-in-law. They were walking in single file, and Zuziwe was in the middle.

Ntabeni greeted all three of them and said, 'Zuziwe, please come and have some tolofiya fruit with me for a while. I won't delay you.'

'Why do you offer tolofiya to Zuziwe alone, bhut' Ntabeni?' asked one of Zuziwe's sisters-in-law with a mischievous smile.

'It's not enough for all three of you,' replied Ntabeni. 'I also wish to speak privately to Zuziwe for a minute. I won't keep her long. Before you reach that bend in the road, we shall have finished eating the tolofiya, and I shall have said what I wish to say. Please, Zuziwe, this is a very small thing I'm asking you to do for me.'

'Bhut' Ntabeni, there's nothing you can say to me which my sisters-in-law may not hear. If you have something to say, say it now, in their presence. Thank you for your offer of tolofiya. If it's not enough for all three of us, you can eat all of it yourself.'

The three women had stopped during this interchange of words. After Zuziwe had spoken, they moved on again. They steadied their buckets with their hands until they regained the rhythm of their walk. Then they balanced the buckets without holding them with their hands.

Ntabeni's heart bled within him. Disappointment, frustration, anger gripped his soul. His scheme had failed. He had wasted his money. The potion was useless. He hurled the tolofiya tin far into the bushes on the side of the footpath. Then he walked slowly back to his home. As he did not wish to meet any people, he avoided the footpath. He walked through the wood, over the rough veld, past the tilled lands, until he reached his hut. He threw himself on his bed and lay there until night set in. He refused to go to the main hut for supper. Zanele brought his supper to his room, but Ntabeni did not touch it despite the combined entreaties of his mother and Zanele. It was close on midnight when he felt he was hungry and tried to eat the mvubo in the dish. It had a bitter taste. He forced himself to swallow a few spoonfuls to dull the sharp edge of hunger. Then he undressed and tried to sleep. Sleep would not come. He lay awake till he became aware of the grey light of dawn entering his room through the small, round, curtained window of his hut. At last he fell asleep. He woke up when his mother shook him violently and told him the day was far advanced. It was no time for dreams. It was time for him to go and tell the boys what had to be done in the fields if he felt he was unable to go out with them.

VIII | *Ntabeni Hits Back*

Three days later Ntabeni went up the Hill of Fools, to a spot on the hilltop which was the favourite rendezvous of the Hlubi boys, especially the bigger ones. The boys liked this spot because it commanded a good view of almost every part of Kwazidenge village. From here they could see their girls as they left their homes to go to the river or the fields or the woods. They could always follow them if they wished and escort them. They could also watch the movements of Thembu boys and girls across the river, but they never interfered with them. The only occasion for contact between Hlubi boys and Thembu boys was a faction fight. There was no need to pursue Thembu girls. There were more than enough girls in Kwazidenge for Hlubi boys. There was no need to dodge the sticks of Thembu boys just because your head had become swollen with love for a Thembu girl. So both the Hlubi boys and the Thembu boys left the enemy girls alone. Very few had ever ventured to pursue an enemy girl throughout the long period of hostility between the two villages. During the last few years not one had attempted it. Not even Diliza, the aggressive Hlubi warrior boy, known and feared by Hlubi and Thembu alike, had been daring enough to venture beyond the Xesi river and taste the Thembu beauties.

No one could remember when the rivalry between the Hlubis and the Thembus began. It was much older than any living man in the two villages. The oldest men remembered vaguely something of the early feuds which had been recounted by their fathers or grandfathers, and the versions differed from family to family. But a common factor in all versions was the Xesi river. The story was told that there was a time when the river was much wider and had more water than it now had. In those days the big boys of the two villages swam regularly in the river pool in summer and held organized swimming contests. The leading warrior boy of the two villages, who was the most skilled at stick-fighting, was always at the head of boys' affairs and automatically took charge of these swimming contests. Boys moved freely from one village to the other and made love to any girl they fancied. The leader always had the best of everything, including girls. But one year there were two bulls, one a Hlubi, the other a Thembu, and they were evenly matched. Their stick-fights always ended in a stalemate. Neither could penetrate the defence of the other. The two bulls quarrelled over the girls and the direction of affairs. The other boys took sides in the dispute, each according to his village. Every swimming contest ended up as a faction fight. Boys went to the Xesi river to fight, not to swim. After a time, the art of swimming was lost and the art of fighting was cultivated. It was many years later that young children took to swimming again, and Thembu and Hlubi youngsters swam together in the river pool. But every boy had to give up the pleasure when he joined the ranks of warrior boys. He had to keep himself ready to fight at all times, and he could not do this if he plunged naked into the river. Besides, the river had grown smaller and was no longer suitable for organized swimming contests. The feud grew increasingly bitter with time and some of the fights ended in death. Sometimes even the men of the two villages joined in the fight. But this was rare, and it was always possible for the older, maturer men to come together and talk the younger out of their violence. This was impossible with the wild, uncircumcised boys. When the boys met at the hilltop, it was as if the world had turned upside down. They became mad, intoxicated maniacs, ready to violate village maids, bully younger boys and rush madly into battle without knowing why they fought.

Ntabeni, bitter at heart because of unrequited love and futile schemes, had decided on a desperate course, to visit the warrior boys at the hilltop. The assembled boys were always dangerous. The villagers expected all sorts of trouble from them. As individuals, most of the boys were pleasant and obedient. If you met one of them in the village, he was quiet and respectful. But when they met on the hilltop, they changed into wild animals. Not even the men of the village had the nerve to go near them. It took much courage for a man to go and talk to them individually or communicate with them as a group.

As Ntabeni approached, he noticed that most of the leading warrior boys were present. He saw Diliza sitting beside his friend, Katana Langa. There was also Ngalweni Nkonde of msenge section, who was the oldest of the warrior boys and was known to be a great fighter. Matshanda and Khanda sat in front, regaling the others with amusing stories, or making fun of the village people and their ways.

These two boys had won fame at the last faction fight when, with three others who had since gone to Rawutini, the gold mines of Johannesburg, they had fought on beside Diliza, even though they knew that the other boys had run away.

'I greet you all,' said Ntabeni, stopping in front of the boys.

'We greet you, bhuti, we greet you, Ntabeni,' replied the boys, some respectfully, others rudely. It was an insult for a boy to call a man by his name. But Ntabeni dared not challenge them for the insult.

'I heard what you were saying about church people, Khanda,' said Ntabeni. 'Do you expect church people to be so very different from other people? They grow thirsty for beer and the other pleasures of life in the same way as those who are not churchgoers. The difference is that church people go to church and pray to God to forgive them for their sins so that they may go to heaven when they die. But the non-converts are also afraid of going to hell even though they refuse to go to church. They always send for a preacher to pray for them when they fear they are about to die.'

'I hear you, bhuti,' replied Khanda. 'I hear and understand. I know that you, for one, like your beer and your church too.' The other boys laughed at Khanda's summary of Ntabeni's character.

'Which would you choose, bhuti,' asked Matshanda, 'if you had to choose between the church on the hill and the beer-house down in the village?'

'The church,' replied Ntabeni, without hesitation. 'I would choose the church. Only I would never refuse the offer of good food. Beer is a very good sort of food after all.'

'And would you still choose the church,' asked Matshanda again, 'if there were no women in it?'

'You will never find such a church. You are more likely to find a church without men than a church without women.'

'With only you, bhuti,' added Khanda, 'to preach to the women and take them home after the evening service?'

'Yes, with only Ntabeni Mlilo and a few faithful men like him to keep the church bells ringing and the church doors open for women and children to go and worship, until the men hear the voice and respond to it.'

'Is there something you want us to do for you, bhuti, that you visit us here today?' asked Diliza, whose curiosity had been roused. He had guessed Ntabeni's business and his guess was not far from the truth. The story of Ntabeni's disappointed love was well known, and he, Diliza, was one of those who suspected that Bhuqa had something to do with it. He himself had been interested in Zuziwe and had been annoyed that a girl who rightly belonged to the big-boy group had to be given up because of a man's offer of marriage. It was downright robbery. But Ntabeni was an important man in the village. So he had been compelled to accept the situation. Now he was partly pleased that Ntabeni was meeting a disappointment similar to his, and partly annoyed that a Thembu boy was receiving a favour which had been denied him by a Hlubi girl.

'Ewe, Diliza, yes, there is. I want you to help me in something which concerns all of you in a way. I have reason to believe that a Thembu boy, Bhuqa, is interfering with the girl I'm planning to marry. I believe he'll try to meet her at the Xesi river, on our side of the river, because there are very few trees on the Thembu side. If he does so, I'd like you to give him a surprise. I'd like you to meet him instead of Zuziwe.'

'How shall we know the time of their appointment that we may keep it also?' asked Ngalweni.

'We are keeping a close watch on Zuziwe's movements. Zanele and Ntombi help me to keep her under observation. I shall send you word as soon as we see them together under the trees near the river.'

'I don't think that will work,' Diliza sneered. 'By the time the message finds us and we reach the spot, they will have finished and the boy will have crossed back to safety. Why don't you attack him at once yourself when you see him interfering with your girl? She's your girl, after all, not ours. Or are you afraid of the boy, bhuti?'

Ntabeni was stung by the insult. Diliza was deliberately mocking him. It was an open challenge. But Ntabeni could not accept it. If he was afraid of Bhuqa, he was also afraid of Diliza. This he admitted to himself. Either of the boys could knead him like clay if he got involved in a fight with them. At such times Ntabeni felt that the responsibility of being a man was too great, for he was compelled to conceal his fear. The world must not know that he, a man, was afraid of an uncircumcised boy. If the secret of his fear became known, he would not be able to live in Kwazidenge. He would have to migrate to a place far away, start a new life there, and create a new image. So he spoke in a blustering tone in reply to Diliza's challenge, though he suspected that most of the boys were not impressed by it.

'No, kwedini,' he heard himself reply in an inadequate

voice, 'I am not afraid of any boy under the sun. You know very well that those boys usually assemble in a group near the ford. I might find myself attacked by many Thembu boys. That's why I've come here to ask you to help me.'

'You are quite right, bhuti,' said Ngalweni. 'Diliza is just teasing you. We are willing to help you. In fact, we shall be doing our duty. It's the duty of Hlubi boys to keep Hlubi territory clear of Thembu boys. Those of us who are near enough will come as soon as you send us word.'

'*Ndiyabulela, madoda*, I thank you, men,' replied Ntabeni, feeling relieved and grateful to Ngalweni for pushing aside Diliza's objections. 'I knew I could rely on you. I don't want this to lead to a faction fight with the Thembu boys, nor do I want a Hlubi boy to be killed because of it. Let Bhuqa alone die. Show him no mercy. I want you to leave him dead on the banks of the Xesi river. That's where his affair with Zuziwe started, I believe. Let it end there. Let him be carried away on a stretcher. After that you can sing a song of triumph over his death. You can hold a feast to celebrate the dog's death and I will pay all the expenses.'

'Now you are speaking, bhuti,' replied Diliza, jumping up with a shout of excitement. Then he stamped hard on the ground, grunting and doing the popular mbhayizelo dance. Several others joined him as he danced to the music of one of the boys, who had pulled out a flute from his pocket and was blowing it as if his life depended on it.

Ntabeni watched them for a little while, pleased that he had persuaded the boys to help him in his plot, and that he would, with one stroke, have his revenge, remove his rival and win back his girl. He walked confidently down the slope and returned home. He did not explain to his sister what he intended doing now that he had failed to serve the love potion. He gave her a vague hint of his intentions so that she might continue to help him spy on Zuziwe. You could not trust a girl with a secret, he believed. Girls and women talked too much. The step he was about to take was dangerous. The boys would be arrested if they killed Bhuqa, as he hoped they would. It must not be known that he had worked out the plot to kill him. He, Ntabeni, must not be known to be involved. He must avoid arrest. He would assist the boys secretly; pay their fines if they were convicted and fined. If the Thembus learnt that a Hlubi man was involved in the killing of Bhuqa, the consequences would be terrible. A faction fight would follow, and it would not be limited to boys. Perhaps war would be declared between the two villages and many people would die. That must be avoided.

Ntabeni walked about near the river ford every day, but took care to keep to the bushes and trees along the riverbank. On one sunny afternoon he lingered among the shadows for several hours, keeping watch on a group of Thembu boys loitering at their favourite spot near the ford. He could not say whether Bhuqa was there or not, but he suspected that he was. The sight of this group of enemy boys fascinated him and made his insides move up to his throat. But nothing happened. Zuziwe did not come. The Thembu boys sat peacefully on the grassy patch till dusk compelled Ntabeni to give up his vigil and return home. He was not discouraged, however. He kept watch for several days. He did not miss one. He did some work on his plot of land in the mornings, or went to morning service if it was a Sunday, to ask God to pour His blessings on him and his, and to pray for a contrite heart and a loving soul. But in the afternoon he never failed to go to the bushes near the river on his mission of hate and vengeance.

About two weeks after Ntabeni had started his spying activities, his efforts were rewarded. From his hiding place he saw Zuziwe walking alone to the river, in the early afternoon. It was unusual for girls to go to the river so early, and alone. She walked briskly, as if she was going on an unusual errand. There was a group of Thembu boys at their usual place. One of these boys left the group and walked along the riverbank, on the Thembu side, apparently without any purpose, for he stopped occasionally to look at the trees near the river, or to follow with his eyes the progress of the river current. When he came opposite a thick cluster of trees which were on the Hlubi side, he went into the water and waded across. The boy was Bhuqa. A thrill of excitement shot through Bhuqa's body, for he had not stepped on enemy soil for a long time. His excitement was increased by the prospect of meeting Zuziwe after the failure of their first appointment since her return from the Thembu village. He heard a slight rustle among the leaves and knew that his loved one was coming to him. They met under the willow tree which Bhuqa had pointed out to her.

Ntabeni hurried to a grazing field near the river where some herdboys were looking after cattle. He sent one of them to the outskirts of Kwazidenge village where he had seen a group of warrior boys, to call them to come to him immediately. He remembered his sister's warning about

Bhuqa's ability as a fighter and did not dare attack him single-handed. The boys came at once and Ntabeni led them towards the unsuspecting lovers. Bhuqa had helped Zuziwe to put down her bucket of water, and they had sat down to enjoy their love for an hour or two. They did not know that a dangerous man, almost mad with jealousy, had been watching them a short distance away. There was as much hatred in Ntabeni's heart as there was love in the hearts of the two lovers.

Diliza was not among the boys who responded to Ntabeni's call, but some of them were famous warriors. Ntabeni whispered to them and ordered three of them to creep softly to the other side so as to cut off Bhuqa's retreat if he decided to run away when they attacked him. He kept the couple under observation so that he might order the three boys who had remained with him to attack at once if Bhuqa realized that he was in danger. When he judged that the three boys had taken up their position on the opposite side, he whispered to the boys who were crouching near him, *'Phambili, madoda!* Forward, men!'

The boys rushed at the two lovers. Bhuqa heard their footsteps, released his hold of Zuziwe and jumped up. He grabbed his stick and turned round to face his enemies. Zuziwe, who had also scrambled to her feet, screamed and told her lover to look behind him. At the precise moment when the first three boys raised their sticks to knock him down, Bhuqa took three long jumps towards the river. He jumped into the water, fully clothed as he was, and tried to swim across. His assailants threw stones at him from the bank. Some stones hit him on his back, and one cut his head. But he pushed on, half swimming, half wading across, till he found shelter behind the trunk of a large tree near the river. It was the Xesi river and that tree trunk which saved him from death. Then Bhuqa took out his whistle and blew it three times. It was a call to his friends to come and help him.

By this time Zuziwe had taken her bucket of water and was walking back to the village as fast as one can walk with an open bucket of water on the head. In her fear and haste she was not careful and much of the water spilt over and soaked her clothes. When she reached home the bucket was only half full. She put it on a table in the kitchen, went to her bedroom, threw herself on her bed and wept. Her anguished sobs shook her whole body, the body she now knew was carrying Bhuqa's baby. She felt a sharp pain in the pit of her stomach. She tried to suppress her sobs, fearing for her baby. Her baby must not be harmed. She owed this to the innocent creature. She must cherish the precious life in her womb. She must live and protect it from all threats of danger. This thought calmed her, and she lay quietly on her bed for a long time.

When the Thembu boys heard Bhuqa's distress call, they picked up their sticks and rushed to his aid. They found him trying to stanch the flow of blood from the cut on his head. His enemies had stopped throwing stones at him, having realized that it was futile trying to hit him behind the cover of the tree trunk. They judged it unwise to follow Bhuqa into enemy territory. They drew inspiration and support for their decision from an ancient proverb, that 'there is joy at the coward's home and sorrow at the brave man's home'.

So they walked away from the river. When they heard the whistle, they knew that Bhuqa was calling for help from his friends, but they did not think that Thembu boys would be foolish enough to cross the river and advance into enemy territory, especially when they learnt that there were Hlubi warrior boys nearby. So the Hlubi boys walked steadily away from the river.

What followed proved their judgement wrong. The sight of Bhuqa's blood infuriated the Thembu boys, and Bhuqa, humiliated by the rough treatment he had received, and incensed by a suspicion of treachery on Zuziwe's part, urged them to pursue the enemy. It was clear that the Hlubi boys had not merely stumbled upon him, but had known of his presence in their territory and had planned their attack: hence his suspicion that Zuziwe had betrayed him.

The Hlubi boys heard them coming. They knew they were heavily outnumbered, and so they decided to run away. At first they trotted steadily, but when they heard the Thembu boys gaining upon them, they ran faster and broke their line formation. They ran so fast that their legs seemed to make a line parallel with the ground. It was as if they wanted to sink their hips into the ground, as the villagers said. Stones flew about their ears and this made them run faster still. They jumped through a fence of dry bramble branches and got themselves badly scratched and their clothes torn. They ran across a field which had recently been ploughed and had been levelled with a harrow by the industrious owner until it was as even as a grass mat. A great deal of time had been spent on it and the work had been done with loving care. But the pursuers and the pursued had neither the time nor the inclination to show appreciation for the husbandry of the honest farmer. They ran across the field and left deep holes in the soft soil. No one heeded the damage to the carefully cultivated land. Every villager was interested in the drama of flight and pursuit. The fighters had full licence to despoil in a moment work which had taken a long time and a great deal of effort to accomplish.

The Hlubi boys were chased by their pursuers until they reached the outskirts of their village. Then the Thembu boys gave up the chase. They went back to the river, crossed over and returned to their village to prepare for the inevitable fight.

IX | *The Blowing Horn*

A wailing, mournful sound was suddenly heard in Kwazidenge. It had a dramatic effect: men, women and children left their work in homes and fields and gathered in small groups all over the village. A small boy, half afraid, half curious, clung to his mother's long flowing skirt and trotted resolutely beside her.

'What is it, mama?' he asked, breathing hard. 'Why are they blowing the horn of death?'

'It's the call to battle, my child. It's the end of the world, as people usually say. Our warrior boys must go and fight the Thembu boys.'

Mother and son joined a small group of villagers.

'What has happened?' she asked the villagers. 'Who started the fight?'

A bearded old villager explained to her, trying to conceal the excitement he felt at the prospect of a faction fight.

'A Thembu boy crossed the Xesi river and tried to rape one of our girls. She was rescued by a group of our own boys. They gave the Thembu boy a thorough beating and the dog would have died the death he deserved if he had not had the presence of mind to blow his whistle, calling for help from his comrades. That boy's ancestors were certainly keeping watch over him because it happened that there was a group of Thembu warrior boys near the river at that very moment and they rushed to help him. Our boys were heavily outnumbered. They ran away. Some would say they did a wise thing. But I say they were stricken with fear like birds.'

The old man paused to take snuff, partly to impress his audience with the importance of the news, partly to hide his own excitement, for it is not manly to show excitement even in a crisis. Women and children may get excited and upset, but a man must be cool at all times and be ready to act with judgement and presence of mind when the need arises.

'I don't know what has happened to our boys,' he continued. 'I really believe their hearts are full of water instead of the good red blood which is the essence of courage. It is not the tradition of Hlubi boys to run away from an enemy, especially when their attackers are the Thembu boys we know, who drink the same water we drink and eat the same food we eat. If the enemy had been strange men from a strange land, backed by spirits with greater power than ours, one would understand our boys running away without striking one blow. But to run away from boys made of the same flesh and blood as they are, sies! It's a disgrace.' The old man spat on the ground in disgust.

'Don't be hard on them, Miya,' pleaded another old man. 'Our boys were a mixed lot. They were not all of the warrior class. Some of them were juniors. It was wise of them to run away. They are still fit and fresh enough to join in the fighting and prove that they are men'.

'Who were the old boys in the group?' asked a third old man. 'I can tell you Diliza was not one of them. I swear by my ancestors Diliza was not in the group. If he had been there, you'd be telling us a different story now.'

'You are right, Radebe,' replied the old man called Miya. 'Diliza was not there.'

'I thought so,' said Radebe triumphantly. 'If he'd been there, there would be a corpse left behind somewhere. And it wouldn't be the corpse of a Hlubi boy. There would be blood and wounds to show. But now, instead of bearing themselves like men, our boys run away to hide like children behind their mothers' skirts, without a drop of blood to prove that they are men.'

'Blood did flow on both sides.' A young man who had been listening respectfully felt constrained to explain. 'Two boys are being treated now by the village doctor in a hut on the outskirts of the village.'

'How did they get hurt if they didn't stand and fight?' asked the old man. 'Did they hit their heads against the tree trunks as they fled in panic?'

'There was some stone-throwing,' explained the young man timidly. 'I think that's how they got hurt.'

'Stone-throwing! We are not Moshweshwe's warriors, who fought their enemy by hurling stones at them. We are not baboons that stand far off and throw objects at their enemy. We come close and cut the enemy down in the manner of Shaka's soldiers.' The disgusted old man moved away from the group and sat on a stone some distance away to await developments.

Zuziwe was still lying on her bed, with her face buried in her pillow, when she heard the horn blowing. She raised her head and listened, and then buried her face again in the soft pillow, a fresh current of tears pouring into the pillow. She who hated fighting was to be the direct cause of a faction fight which might lead to the death of an innocent boy. O God, she prayed involuntarily, let it not be Bhuqa who dies. Dear God, please forgive me for my selfish prayer, and please watch over Bhuqa. Let him not die, God. Save the father of my unborn child.

Zuziwe heard Duma and two of her sisters-in-law speaking outside, excited.

'At last our boys have decided to teach those Thembu boys a lesson,' said Duma. 'It's a long time since we had a faction fight. Those Thembus were becoming over-bold. I have been told that one of them stole across the Xesi river and was caught by our boys. He's lucky to have escaped death. It's a pity our boys were armed only with sticks. If they had hit that dog with knobkerries or chopped him with battle-axes, he would have died long before his friends came to rescue him.'

Zuziwe shut her ears. She did not wish to hear any more. She felt a pain in her stomach, as if the pangs of birth were come. But she knew that they were still far off. She expected Duma to enter her room and curse her for what she had done. But he did not.

Within a few minutes of the sounding of the horn, Hlubi boys, fully armed with nailed knobkerries, sticks and battle-axes, moved swiftly and silently to the top of the Hill of Fools. Zuziwe heard Duma raise his voice to speak to Katana Langa, who was hurrying past on his way to the hilltop.

'Hurry up, Katana,' said Duma, 'and fight well. I want to see a dead Thembu on the battlefield after the fight.'

'I mean to do some work down there, bhuti,' replied Katana, speaking in his usual husky voice. 'It won't be just one dead Thembu, I promise you that.' He moved on.

Duma waited a long time, speaking to the women on the prospects of the fight, and varying his comments with remarks to other warrior boys who walked past. He moved up and down on the sun-scorched grass, like a madman in a cage. He could not restrain his excitement. But poor Zuziwe's grief burnt inside her body and dried up the saliva in her mouth, making it taste like ash.

The boys waited for two hours for the full complement of warriors. Some were delayed by the tears and entreaties of sisters and mothers who were urging them to stay at home and keep out of the fight. But very few boys who were frequenters of the Hill of Fools could ignore the blowing horn. They had been taught to believe that the horn called on them to defend their homes and their families. Thembu boys must be taught to keep away from Hlubi boys or girls. They must not trespass on Hlubi territory.

All the villagers were waiting expectantly for Diliza to join the warriors, for he was famous for his bravery. Young and old remembered his feats in numerous faction fights and in single encounters with other boys. Was it not he who fought and beat the bully of the Hlubi village even before he was a full-grown boy of the warrior class? Was it not he who alone faced and beat off two Thembu boys when they surprised him near the Xesi river at dusk one summer's day? Even grey-haired old men could not contain their excitement when they described how he saved the day for the Hlubis at the last faction fight. He and five others stood and fought so bravely that their comrades, who had run away, returned and gave support to the six heroes till the enemy was beaten off. Yes, the villagers and the warriors were waiting confidently for Diliza to come.

But his mother, his sisters and even his aged father were making things difficult for him. They were in great fear for him for they knew his utter recklessness in the heat of battle. They remembered vividly his narrow escape at the last fight. His father was refusing to give him his knobkerrie and his blessing, and Diliza valued the latter with the intensity of a simple mind. His two sisters clung to him, one on each arm, and tried to hold him back by force. His mother was frantic with grief. One moment she cursed herself for having given birth to a heartless male child. Next moment she went down on her knee and begged him to have mercy on his mother. Then, again she threatened to poison herself rather than die of a broken heart. Diliza was upset, but he could not give in. He knew that his failure to answer the call to arms would be a betrayal of his comrades, and that the village would see it as a national calamity.

'Tell me, tata,' he asked, 'how would you like it if your son were hounded out of the village as a coward?'

'That would be bad indeed, my son. But your mother and I would bear it better than losing our only son. Moreover, they all know in this village that you are not a coward. I, your father, forbid you to join this senseless fighting. I shall let everyone know that the fault is not yours, if you stay at home. I have always spoken up strongly against these faction fights at our village meetings. It's those counsellors who have no sons involved who have always opposed me and said that the fights are good military training for the boys. It's all nonsense. Why should the boys be given military training if we intend to live at peace with one another? Listen to me, my son, I beg you. Stay at home today, just this once, for I have a strange feeling in me. I'm almost certain that today's fight will produce at least one death, and that may be yours.'

'Tata, forgive me. I can't do it. If you can stop the fights, I shall accept that, perhaps with some regret, but I assure you I shall accept it. However, if you Hlubi greybeards, with all your wisdom, cannot agree in your village meetings to stop the fights, we boys of fighting age have no choice but to go to war. Give me my knobkerrie please, tata, or would you have me go and fight only with this stick?'

'No, no, my son.' The old man gave in. 'Take your knobkerrie and use it well. And may the spirits of our ancestors go with you and protect you.'

Diliza took his knobkerrie and broke loose from his sisters. He looked at his tearful mother, turned sharply and ran steadily to the hilltop. The first among the waiting villagers to see him was an old counsellor, famous in his day for his prowess and dexterity with the stick. He had been keeping his eye fixed on the path leading to Diliza's home. He broke into praise-song, half-spoken, half-sung:

> 'Like a lion in the bush when it speeds towards its prey
> Comes Diliza the brave, comes Diliza the swift,
> With his sharp axe and his club and his knobkerrie raised;
> Who can withstand the full force of his blow?'

The poet went on in this strain without pausing for breath until Diliza joined the band of warriors on the hilltop. His arrival had a dramatic effect. The tense silence changed into a bustle of activity. Weapons were tested. Belts were tightened. Women ululated. Dogs barked. The sound of the horn became loud and clear. It changed from the mournful note of catastrophe to a brighter note of confidence and encouragement.

The Hlubi boys were about to leave the hilltop when a boy came running towards them. He was Mlenzana Nqaba of msenge section. His story was the opposite of Diliza's. He and Mlungisi Nkabi, also of msenge section, had been sitting on a large stone in the sinquma woodland beyond the village when the horn sounded. They were looking after a herd of cattle.

'There goes the horn, Mlungisi,' said Mlenzana. 'It means that all Hlubi boys must go and fight the Thembus.'

'I can't go,' said Mlungisi. 'There will be trouble for our boys if I go and fight.'

'Why?' asked Mlenzana.

'As I was heading back two cows which were going the wrong way at the edge of the forest, I saw a dead black cat with staring eyes right in front of me. If I go and fight without being doctored, I shall bring our boys bad luck. One of our own Hlubi boys may be killed and we may even lose the fight. I can't go.'

'Do you believe this? Are you certain it will be one of our boys who will be killed and not a Thembu boy?'

'It must be a Hlubi boy. The dead cat was lying right on my path and it seemed to be staring at me with an eye of death. At first I thought it meant death in my family. I had decided to report this to my father so that he might do something to ward off the evil. But now I know it must mean that one of our boys will die unless I keep away.'

'Don't you know what will happen to you if you stay away from the fight?' asked Mlenzana.

'Yes, I know,' replied Mlungisi. 'I know that I shall be insulted and persecuted by the other boys and by the village people. But they will understand and agree with me when they know the reason. I'll take some men to the spot so that they may see the dead cat with their own eyes if they wish. But what about you, Mlenzana? You don't seem to be keen to go and fight. Are you afraid?'

'No, I'm not afraid. But I don't like to fight when there's no reason for fighting.'

'There must be a reason. If you go to the hilltop where the boys are, or to the village, you'll find out what has happened. There must be a good reason.'

'Then this would be the first faction fight fought with a good reason. All the other fights I've known were fought for nothing. The boys fight because the blood is flowing too strongly in their veins and they want to let some of it out.'

After a while the two boys heard the voices of some men. They judged that the men were coming towards them because the voices became more and more distinct. There were four men. Mlenzana's stepmother, suspecting Mlenzana of cowardice, had asked some relatives to go and look for him and make him go and join the other boys in the fight. Mlenzana's real name was Xolile, but the other boys had nicknamed him 'Mlenzana', which meant 'he-of-the-legs', because he always went away when a fight broke out between them. The nickname had gradually taken the place of the real name. Mlenzana was an orphan. His mother had died when he was only ten years of age, and his father had re-married two years later. Mlenzana's father had died when Mlenzana was sixteen years of age. His stepmother hated him. She did not even try to hide her hatred. Mlenzana on his part had no ill-feelings towards his stepmother. He lived with her and her three young sons, his half-brothers, even though he could have left and gone to live with an uncle at Jojo village, or with his father's twin brother at Kwazidenge. Mlenzana was of great help to his stepmother, but she did not appreciate this. She made a big fuss over the smallest mistake he made.

The men had been searching for Mlenzana for some time. They were in a bad mood. Their anger increased when they found him comfortably seated on the stone. His malume, a brother to his stepmother, went up to him in a threatening manner.

'What are you doing here, kwedini Mlenzana?' he asked.

'You can see I'm looking after these cattle,' replied the boy, jumping down from the stone.

'Are you cheeky with me, kwedini?' shouted his malume angrily, and followed up his words with a sharp blow on Mlenzana's thighs.

Mlenzana's bawokazi intervened. 'Don't hit him, Miya,' he said. 'We want him to go and join the other boys. Kwedini,' he continued, addressing Mlenzana, 'leave the cattle here. Come with us. You must fetch your weapons and fight.'

'I don't want to fight,' mumbled Mlenzana. 'Those Thembu boys have done nothing to me. Why should I fight them?'

'This boy is dreaming,' said his malume angrily. 'His cowardice makes him talk like a madman.'

'But, malume—'

'Kwedini, thula! If you say one word more, I'll knock you down like the dog you are. I think our boys will be better off fighting without you. I fear you'll infect them with your cowardice. You should be ashamed of yourself.'

'Mlenzana, my child, the Thembus are old enemies of ours,' explained his bawokazi patiently. 'Today one of them raped a Hlubi girl. Then they violated our territory and attacked our boys. They must not be allowed to do that. If you boys don't fight them, they'll think you are afraid of them, and do worse things. They might even attack our women and children and beat up old men. Then where will the Hlubi people find safety if they can't find it in their own village? All the boys of your age will never be respected by the villagers if that happens. You'll be scorned and hissed at as cowards. You'll not be able to lay down the law in your old age. Children not yet born will be told the story of your cowardice. Be careful then what you do. Go and fight.'

'Stop wasting time talking to this boy, Maduna,' burst in Mlenzana's malume, who had been listening impatiently to the long speech. 'This boy is dreaming. It's cowardice which makes him say all this nonsense.'

'What about you, Mlungisi?' asked Nqaba, Mlenzana's bawokazi, turning to the other boy. 'Why are you sitting here? Why don't you go and fight? Has Mlenzana persuaded you also to keep away?'

'Hayi, bawo, no, not at all. I have a very good reason for not fighting. When we heard the horn blowing I told Mlenzana I couldn't go and fight. I shall help our boys better by keeping out of it.'

'What do you mean?' asked Nqaba. 'What riddle are you speaking? This is no time for riddles. This is a matter of life and death. Blood will soon flow, perhaps to be followed by death. Speak in direct, plain language, not in riddles.'

'I'm quite serious, bawo Nqaba. I told Mlenzana before you came, and I tell you now: I saw a dead black cat right in my path at the edge of the wood earlier today. It was staring at me with its lifeless eyes. I didn't know at the time what it meant. At first I thought it meant death in my family. When I heard the sound of the horn, I knew at once it meant the death of a Hlubi boy and the defeat of the Hlubis. I knew that the only way to avert disaster would be for me to keep out of the fight. I'm glad you have come, for now I can take you to the dead cat. When you have seen it with your own eyes, then you can be witnesses to my story before the village people.'

'*Kulungile*, it's all right, Mlungisi,' said Nqaba. 'Two of us will go with you and see the cat, and the other two will go back with Mlenzana. If your story is true, then you will be commended for your action by the men of the village. A dead cat is an evil thing. It would have brought bad luck on our boys. Perhaps your father will decide to take you to a sanuse at once. Let's hurry. There's so much to do and no time to lose.'

Mlungisi went with two men to the spot where the cat still lay on the narrow path in the wood. They satisfied themselves that it was dead and black and that it was staring in the direction from which Mlungisi had come. They stood a good distance away from the cat and avoided the side at which it was staring. They did not wish to bring death to their families. They ordered Mlungisi to take it by its hind leg and throw it into a thick bush away from the path. Then they went back to the village.

The men gave Mlungisi's father a detailed account of the event. Nkabi was partly relieved and partly upset by the report. Some boys had called at his home on their way to the hilltop and had been disappointed that Mlungisi had not yet responded to the battle-call. He knew what would happen if his son failed the other boys in this moment of crisis. So he was relieved that Mlungisi had a good reason for keeping out of the fight and that there were responsible men to support his story. But now what about the evil itself? That worried him. If the disaster was averted from the Hlubi warriors, what course would it take? Was his family safe? He decided to act at once. He thanked the men for having taken the trouble to investigate his son's report. He asked them to complete their good work by telling as many villagers as possible about the dead cat and the reason why his son did not join the other boys. He ordered Mlungisi to prepare for a journey to Jojo village, to the home of Gabulamehlo, the great sanuse, who would know how to avert disaster. And so it happened that at the very time when Mlenzana was joining the band of Hlubi warriors at the hilltop, Mlungisi, his father and two male relatives were setting out on horseback on their four-mile journey to Jojo village.

The sanuse saw them coming. He ordered his assistant Mathambo to meet them outside and guide them to the visitors' hut, the hut in which he divined, in which he looked back into the past and far into the future, in which he revealed the truth to his anxious clients, in which he tried to understand the mysteries of nature, of life and death, in which he was daring enough, like all men of medicine, to attempt to control the fates of men and to alter the course of events by the manipulation of his roots and herbs. Mathambo knew his job and did it well. Mathambo's preliminary examination and report usually helped his chief to appear uncannily accurate when he himself went to the visitors to divine.

The wise one came in, dressed in full ceremonial costume. He was preceded by six novitiates, all women, who came in singing and clapping hands and stamping on the ground to the rhythm of their song. He himself did not sing. He stamped on the ground and performed a variety of movements with his arms, his legs and his head. His dark mystic eyes were deepened by the grotesque paintings on his face, which inspired the onlookers with awe. He made a strange sound once, as if he was sneezing, and the singing stopped abruptly. Then he stopped suddenly in front of the visitors and glared at them.

'*Bantu basemzini*, strangers from a far land, you want the truth revealed to you, *vumani*, confirm!' shouted Gabulamehlo in a voice like that of a man in a nightmare, waving his ox-tail.

'*Siyavuma!* We confirm!' responded the visitors.

'*Bantu basemzini*, you bid me speak, *vumani!*' said the wise one again.

'*Siyavuma! Siyavuma!*'

'The business which brings you here concerns a man, *vumani!*'

'*Siyavuma! Siyavuma!*' responded the visitors doubtfully.

'*Hayi, ndaxoka!* No, I'm lying! It concerns a boy, *vumani!*'

'*Siyavuma! Siyavuma!*' responded the visitors with more enthusiasm. The sanuse felt he had hit upon the truth. So he snorted and the novitiates burst into blood-stirring song. He danced and strutted up and down the hut, nodding, gesturing. He snorted again. The singing stopped.

'It concerns a boy. It concerns the boy's family. *Vumani!*'

'*Siyavuma! Siyavuma!*' responded the visitors, almost screaming with excitement.

'It concerns the boy in this room now. *Vumani!*'

'*Siyavuma! Siyavuma!*'

'It is a matter of life and death in the boy's family. *Vumani!*'

'*Siyavuma! Siyavuma!*' came the enthusiastic response.

'You want death to be driven away. *Vumani!*'

'*Siyavuma! Siyavuma!*' shouted the visitors more forcefully than before.

'*Phosa ngasemva, ugqibile!* Throw behind, you have finished,' added Nkabi, shouting louder than the others.

The sanuse snorted. The novitiates took up their singing and hand-clapping again. They jumped up and joined their chief, who was going through a variety of movements round the hut. After completing a few circles Gabulamehlo sat down suddenly in front of the visitors. The novitiates completed their singing and dancing and sat at the back of the hut. The sanuse looked at Nkabi, smiling, satisfied at the successful outcome of his divination.

'Let your arm lift us up, wise one,' said Nkabi. 'We appeal to you to proceed with this matter which you in your wisdom have found out.'

'I am your tool,' replied Gabulamehlo. 'Do what you will with me.'

The sanuse and the novitiates went out of the hut, leaving the visitors alone. After a while the sanuse came back and gave Mlungisi a small dark object.

'Here, boy,' he said, 'take this root and chew it. It is a powerful root. You must keep it in your mouth for three days, except when you go to bed. You, Nkabi, must sprinkle your yard, especially the entrance to each hut and to the cattle-kraal, with a mixture which I will prepare for you while my assistants give you food to eat. Then the evil will be driven away from your family.'

The sanuse did not keep them waiting long. He brought in a tin full of a reddish liquid which he covered with a tight-fitting lid after he had shown it to Nkabi. One of the novitiates gave them a dish of boiled mealies. She came in again and gave them a tin full of sour milk. They enjoyed the sour milk. It helped to wash down the mealies, which they had not enjoyed. Nkabi was told to pay four goats or twenty-four rand for the sanuse's services. He paid down half of this amount in money and promised to send the balance next day in the form of two goats.

X | *Faction Fight*

Mlenzana went home with the two men at a stiff pace. His bawokazi feared that the company of Hlubi warriors would leave the hilltop before Mlenzana arrived. They could still hear the horn blowing. They were quite close to the village, but not yet within sight of it, when they heard the blowing horn change from the mournful note of crisis to a brighter note of confidence.

'The warriors are ready to go down,' said Nqaba. 'I can make it out from the tone of the horn. You are late, Mlenzana. It's always dangerous to be late for a faction fight. You may be as late as you like for a wedding or a funeral, but never for a faction fight. It's bad to be late for this sort of engagement. Let's hurry. It will tire you, I know, and you have some strenuous fighting to do. You will need all your strength. But it can't be helped. We must hurry. You must not be late for the work you have to do. You must be there when the fight starts, otherwise you won't know what tactics your side is using. You won't know who is fighting next to you, whom to support. You won't be able to distinguish between friend and foe, especially when the battle-formation is broken, as so often happens. And you may be knocked down whilst peering into the faces of the fighting warriors. Here we are. We have arrived at last. Go in and take your weapons and run quickly to the hilltop.'

They had indeed arrived at Mlenzana's home. His stepmother fired a volley of curses at Mlenzana when he entered the hut.

'*Gwalandini!* You coward!' she shouted at him. 'Do you think I shall cook for a coward? You got your cowardice from your mother, you worm! You cowdung! You human refuse! You didn't get it from my husband. You won't sleep in my hut if you don't go and fight, I tell you.'

Mlenzana paid no attention to his stepmother. She went on cursing even after he had left the hut. She sent the curses after him as he trotted off. Mlenzana's bawokazi tried to intervene.

'*Myeke*, let him be, woman,' he said. 'I spoke strongly to him in the wood. It's enough. He's not made of stone. He has heard us. He needs our good wishes now that he is going to the battlefield. If you swear at him by his mother, you are removing the soil from under his feet and he will be left hanging in air. You ought to support him now like a mother. Don't destroy him.'

'What are you talking about, Maduna? I don't understand you. Are you defending that coward?'

'No, mfazi, I'm not defending him. I'm appealing to you to be kind to your husband's child. He's hungry for love. Don't feed him with curses. But I've spoken enough. I didn't come for this. I came to save the boy from public disgrace. I'm glad I was successful in that.'

Nqaba turned round and walked away from his sister-in-law. She stood looking at him until he disappeared behind a cluster of msenge trees. Her breast was heaving and a flood of anger was welling up in her heart.

'What does he think he is?' she said to herself. 'Does he think he's going to bully me in my own house? And for the sake of that coward? Never!'

Meanwhile Mlenzana had joined the Hlubi band of warriors at the hilltop, arriving just when they were about to move down to the battlefield. The boys moved silently through the village. Then they formed a semi-circle and trotted slowly to the rhythm of their battle-song which they sang softly as they advanced. They stopped about two hundred yards away from the battlefield. Diliza, their leader, outlined his plan of attack. He, with nine veterans and twenty juniors, would be in the centre of the semi-circle. Six veterans and twelve juniors would hold each wing to prevent the Thembu boys from encircling them. If for some reason it became necessary to withdraw, he would blow his whistle twice. Then they must all retire quickly but keep together.

The Thembu boys had gathered at their favourite spot near the river. They had soon grown into a formidable force. The boys of fighting age had been trained to hold themselves ready for action at any time. They crossed the river by the bridge of stones and formed themselves up in battle array under the direction of their leader, Bhuqa. His open wound showed clearly on his head. The hair near the wound had been carefully removed with a razor blade and an ointment applied to it. There was neither bandage nor plaster over it.

The valley was bathed in glorious sunshine as the two

companies stood poised for action. A gentle breeze fanned the leaves of the mealie plants in the fields adjoining the battlefield. Small insects rushed up and down, building houses or laying by stores for themselves and their young ones. Field rats peeped cautiously from their burrows, came out and scurried across from one hideout to another. Birds in the trees along the river sang full-throatedly in appreciation of the glories of nature. A hawk which had been flying high in the sky suddenly plunged and pandemonium broke loose in the world of chickens. A hen shouted a word of warning and dashed to safety, followed by all her young ones. But not quite all. The hawk soared to the sky again, clutching a screaming, helpless chick in its sharp claws. From the safety of a thick bush a cock hurled defiance at the hawk. It was a black day in this community of fowls. The hen grieved over the loss of her young one and the cock hung his head with shame at his failure to protect his family. The other chicks panted with fear and were quite bewildered by the strange events.

The green field which was to be the scene of fierce fighting belonged to one of the Hlubi villagers. It had once been arable land. It had been left fallow for several years and had become a grazing field for the owner's cows. There was a public road on one side of the field and the Xesi river served as the boundary on the opposite side. The ground was uneven in some places, as if it had been ploughed but had not been harrowed when it was last tilled. The spot where the fighting took place was quite even and covered with short grass, as though it was specially kept neat and prim for the occasion by a keen gardener. The owner was a strict man who allowed no nonsense on his land. No boys ever held stick fights there. They never trespassed on it. The cows always grazed unmolested, serving as lawn-mowers which kept the field ready for faction fights.

It was strange that the owner never raised any objection to the faction fights fought at this spot. The Hlubis and the Thembus seemed to regard the field as the official battlefield. When the Thembu warriors crossed the river and moved up to the battlefield, it was generally understood that they were within their rights. No one questioned their right to use the bridge of stones, even though it was known that the bridge had been built to facilitate peaceful communication. It was unthinkable that they could be stopped at the ford by the men of either village. No policemen interefered. The Hlubi men and other non-combatants stood on the slope of the Hill of Fools and watched the drama with keen interest, while the Thembu non-combatants stood beyond the river, on the stony ground which sloped from their village towards the river. It was a perfect, natural stadium, suitable for combatants and spectators alike.

Somehow, the cows were never in the way when there was a fight. Was it a coincidence that they were always grazing away from the arena whenever human beings were butchering one another? Was it some mysterious, supernatural force which moved the beasts away so that the human animals might indulge their animal instincts to the full? The cows always returned to the field afterwards and grazed on the grass with the unconcern of a man watching a beast being slaughtered at the abattoir. The human blood with which the grass had been watered did not trouble them, but if it had been the blood of another cow, they would have been quite upset. They would have groaned and screamed and roared and made a great deal of noise, as men often do when a friend or a relative dies. The cows always grazed on the grass and the peasant who owned them always drank their milk as if nothing had happened on the grazing field.

The leader of each of the opposing bands gave the word to attack and the two groups rushed at each other. The Thembu boys' formation was in the shape of a wedge. Leading the attack was a tall, hefty, left-handed boy nicknamed Nxele, who came straight at Diliza. The two warriors met with the ferocity of two bulls. Neither of them gained the advantage. Their duel was interrupted by their supporters, who were eager to exchange blows with the famous warriors and win glory for themselves. The fighting increased in intensity. Some combatants hammered at the heads of their adversaries with the nail-studded knobkerrie, while others dealt out terrible blows with the battle-axe. A stout stick held in the left hand of each fighter was used as a sort of shield to ward off the enemy's blows. Whenever a comrade was knocked down, his friends rushed to his aid and stood over him until he was able to rise and continue the fight. Blood flowed freely and the fighting grew increasingly fierce. Some blows landed. Others ended in the air. Gaping wounds were made with the battle-axe and large lumps appeared on the human head when the murderous knobkerrie landed. It was indeed a miracle that warriors' skulls remained uncrushed by the terrible weapon.

After twenty minutes, Diliza and the warriors round him began to master their opponents who were bleeding freely and losing ground. The left flank of the Hlubis, under the leadership of Ngalweni, was holding its ground against a determined Thembu attack. But the Hlubi right flank was gradually giving ground. Bhuqa saw that this was the weak spot of the Hlubi front line. So he sent five experienced warriors to the spot to increase the pressure. Diliza was about to send some of the veterans near him to the right flank when disaster struck his group. A sharp, piercing sound was heard above the noise of battle. It came from the whistle of the Thembu left-hander, who was facing Diliza and his veterans. It was a sign that he was in trouble and needed help. But as the sound came from the spot where Diliza was fighting, the Hlubis took it as the signal for retreat and ran to a knoll some three hundred yards away to regroup and await further instructions. The Thembus were surprised at this sudden withdrawal. Bhuqa suspected a trap. He restrained those fighters in his group who were wanting to follow up their victory. A short, thickset boy who had been the head and inspiration of the victorious Thembu flank was furious. He spoke up strongly and almost insultingly against Bhuqa's decision.

'Are you so frightened of Diliza,' he raged, 'that you fear to chase him even when he runs away? Let me face him if you find him too rough for you. I tell you, man, when a boy runs away, he won't turn back if he hears footsteps behind him.'

'Take care, Dabula. Be careful what you say. I'm the leader here. If you want my place, come and fight me for it here and now. I may be afraid of Diliza, as you say, but I'm not afraid of you.'

'*Hayi, bafondini!* Cool down and prepare for the fight,' said a blood-spattered boy. 'Those Hlubi boys are not yet beaten, and they never will be, as long as Diliza is on his legs. Look at them forming up on that knoll. This is no time to quarrel among ourselves.'

'That's just what I say,' answered Bhuqa. 'Their retreat was a trick to draw us into a trap. I refuse to fall into the trap. Now, men, take your places and be on your guard. Here they come.'

After they had run to the knoll, which Diliza had been the last to reach, the Hlubi boys had sat down dejected and ashamed at having run away. They could not understand why their leader had given the signal to retreat. Their spirits were revived when Diliza explained the mishap. Fresh plans were discussed and preparations for another attack made. Matshanda and Khanda were transferred from the centre to the right flank in an effort to strengthen this flank. Mlenzana was moved from the left flank to the centre to fill the gap caused by the removal of these veterans. The warriors dried their bloody hands and the bloody handles of their weapons on the grass.

Then Diliza, speaking in a strong voice, said: 'Madoda! This is one of the toughest fights I have ever fought against the Thembus. Our victory will be a credit to us. Of course we shall win. If we go and fight determined to die rather than run away, then we must win. We are heavily outnumbered, it is true. But that has happened to us before. Let us fight together and give each other full support. Let each blow find its mark. Then we shall certainly come out victorious.' Then the Hlubi regiment rushed at the Thembus again.

It was late afternoon and the light was failing on the low-lying battlefield. But the glorious peak of the high Bhukazana mountain was still suffused with the pale rays of the setting sun. The lofty mountain was untouched by the gale that was sweeping the humble valley below the Hill of Fools. The clouds floated on and sped to other parts of the universe, untouched by the storm. But for the Thembus and the Hlubis the drama was painfully real. Some were afraid but others were tense with excitement.

Zuziwe had rushed out when Duma shouted with dismay that the Hlubi boys were running away. She was not upset by the defeat of the Hlubis. She told Duma's wife that she was pleased no one had been killed. Duma heard her remark and turned round on her.

'Don't rejoice too early, girl,' he said. 'I know on which side your sympathies are. But the fight has not ended yet. Our boys have not run away. They are regrouping. The Thembus have not followed them. It means that the Thembus have received such rough handling that they do not wish to go near our boys if they can help it. Don't be too quick to rejoice. You may still find a corpse on your lap instead of a lover. Look at our boys making their ox-horn formation. That must be Diliza standing in front of them. Yes, he is about to lead them forward again! Yes, they are rushing at the enemy and, would you believe it, the Thembus are standing still, thoroughly sated with the broiled meat, as the saying goes!'

Zuziwe did not like being a spectator, but she was fascinated by the spectacle in spite of herself. The growing darkness made it difficult for them to see what was happening. She heard the clash of arms when the combatants met again and felt a shock as if one of the blows was landing on Bhuqa, who, she knew, was somewhere in the front line of the Thembu company. She thought of her baby, wondering what she would do if its father was killed. So she prayed again that Bhuqa might live and marry her and make her child legitimate.

For a full fifteen minutes the fight went on. Dabula and other Thembu warriors concentrated their attack on the spot where Diliza was fighting. Neither side could master the other. One Thembu flank was led by Bhuqa and the other by the left-hander, Nxele. Their plan was to overwhelm the Hlubi flanks and then turn round, encircle and disorganize the enemy, their greater numbers making these tactics possible. Their plan succeeded. The Hlubi ranks did become disorganized. Their fighting became ineffective and many of them were knocked down. They panicked and failed to keep together. In the growing darkness most of them decided that life, even without glory, was preferable to a glorious death. They ran away.

But the centre of the Hlubi front fought on, despite the overwhelming odds. Katana Langa, who was fighting bravely though completely surrounded by Thembu warriors, was dealt a mighty blow with a knobkerrie by Bhuqa and bit the dust. Soon after that Diliza, Mlenzana and three other boys were left alone, almost completely surrounded by the enemy. It was growing darker and darker. It was unlikely that the boys who had run away would see what was happening and return to rescue their comrades.

Diliza, unnerved by the darkness and by his inability

to distinguish friend from foe, shouted to his supporters to follow him as he fought his way out and, for the first time in his life, ran away. He probably remembered what his elders used to say: 'There is laughter at the coward's home and tears at the brave man's home'.

Bhuqa decided that it was unwise to allow his warriors to spread out in the growing darkness and chase the fleeing Hlubis. A leader had to be cautious where the Hlubis were concerned. So he called the Thembus back. On their way back, as they passed the dying Katana, who was lying on the ground bleeding from a cracked skull, each of the Thembu boys hit him on the head, to make certain that the guilt of killing him was shared by all of them. Then they crossed the river again by the bridge of stones and returned to their village.

The Hlubi boys ran back to their village and re-assembled at the hilltop. They felt too ashamed to meet the villagers, preferring each other's company as comrades in disgrace. When Diliza re-joined them, he was furious. He wanted to wipe out the defeat from his memory and perhaps even clear his name by attacking somebody else. He wanted the blame to be brought home to the boys who had run away first. He subjected each boy to a thorough cross-examination. Each had to give an account of his conduct during the fight and it had to be corroborated by the boys who had been fighting near him. Some of the bigger boys resented this and made a counterimagecharge against him.

'It was your leadership which caused our defeat,' said Ngalweni. 'It was quite clear that the Thembu boys were trying to encircle us, and you did nothing to prevent it.'

'I suppose you think you could have led our boys better than I, Ngalweni,' said Diliza with an ugly sneer. 'But the point is, did you run away first or last?'

'You seem to be proud of the fact that you ran away last. You are as much of a coward as those who ran away first, if it's cowardice to run away. We have always been told that you would rather die than run away. Why are you not lying dead on the battlefield if you are so brave?'

'Stop blaming each other for something that cannot be mended,' said Mlenzana. 'Are you aware there's somebody missing? Katana is not here. I have been looking for him. He's definitely not here. He was one of those who remained behind fighting. We were hard pressed and he was separated from us. I don't know what's happened to him.'

All the boys were shocked when they realized that Katana was indeed missing. They searched for him, but it was too dark to see. They called out his name several times. There was no response. Two boys went to his home hoping that he had gone straight there. But they knew in their hearts that only death or serious disablement could prevent a warrior boy from going to the hilltop after a fight. The assembly broke up and each boy went back to his own home.

Dark silence settled over the battleground. The dead body of Katana, with its staring, bulging eyes, remained the sole watcher of the night. After a while a few shadowy figures came slowly onto the field, searching for the boy who had been reported missing, and probably dead. On finding the cold corpse of his son, Katana's father, a younger brother of Mvangeli Langa, broke down and wept. Deep, heart-rending sobs shook his body. His companions tried to comfort him. He would not be comforted. After some time he calmed down and gave an order in a husky voice that they should proceed. The corpse was placed on a crude stretcher made of thin poles held together by strips of ox-leather. Four men lifted up the stretcher and the ghostly procession moved slowly to the Hlubi village. When the men brought the corpse into the hut where the anxious mother sat and waited, she was so shocked that she went numb. She did not cry, nor did she utter a single word. She merely stared unseeing and glassy-eyed at the body of her child who would never again speak to her, nor father her grandchildren, nor be her support in her old age.

Diliza was humbled by the outcome of the fight. For the next few days he did not leave his home. He could not go out and meet villagers whom he had always known to be full of praise for him, and who would now look at him with contempt. He was completely cured of the lunacy which he had caught like a fever on the crest of the Hill of Fools. The end of wildness and violence had come. After three days he went to the recruiting agency at Qoboqobo where he signed a contract to go and work in a Johannesburg gold mine for nine months. This marked the end of his term as leader of the warrior boys and of his participation in faction fighting.

XI | *Funeral*

On the day after the fight Mlenzana went to Mlungisi's home, where he was told that Mlungisi had been given the task of going round Kwazidenge to announce the death of Katana. Mlenzana met Mlungisi on his way to Mvangeli's house and joined him. Mvangeli and Duma were away from home, so the two boys were received by Zuziwe and Duma's wife. Both women broke down and wept when the death was announced, even though they had already heard of it. Duma had learnt of it during the night and had passed on the sad news to the rest of the family. Zuziwe's grief was sharpened by a feeling of guilt, by the knowledge that the village people would accuse her and condemn her for having caused the boy's death, and most of all by the realization that the baby in her womb formed a strong tie between her and Bhuqa, whereas the death of Katana separated them with a finality that was frightening.

On their way to other homes, Mlungisi told Mlenzana about the visit to the sanuse and the successful outcome of the sanuse's divination.

'Why do you say it was successful?' asked Mlenzana. 'You might as well have gone to the fight to help us. Your staying away didn't help. Your presence might have helped us to defeat the Thembus. We were outnumbered. Another pair of arms might have made the difference.'

'The defeat of our boys was not the sanuse's fault. He was not asked to doctor the Hlubi warriors but to drive evil away from my family. He did what he was required to do. Our warriors should have been properly doctored before they went out to fight and they would have resisted the evil witches of Kwazidenge.'

Mlenzana laughed. 'I see there's no way of shaking you out of your belief,' he said. 'I suppose you are right. If our boys had been doctored, perhaps they would have had more confidence in themselves and they would not have run away.'

During the next few days the relatives, friends and neighbours of the bereaved family came to condole with the grief-stricken parents. Zuziwe spent most of her time at the home of 'the brother she had sent to his death', as some villagers told her. She helped to serve black tea or coffee to the mourners and to wash dishes. There were many women who came to help. The attitude of most of them towards Zuziwe was unpleasant, and even hostile. They would not speak to her, but they spoke about her so that she could hear, completely condemning her. The presence of her mother and Duma's wife saved her from open insult. Duma's wife tried to protect Zuziwe by keeping her away from the hut and the fireplace where most of the women were working. She kept Zuziwe in the main hut, serving the mourners and clearing the table when they finished their coffee-and-bread meal. It was much better for her to work in the main hut where there were men, always kinder to a woman in trouble than other women. But Zuziwe was afraid of her bawokazi, Katana's father. She avoided him whenever she could, though he himself took no notice of her. The only man who was outspoken in condemning Zuziwe was Ntabeni. He seemed to be speaking about her whenever she passed near him. But the men who listened to him appeared to be more attracted by the girl than resentful of her.

Very little work was done in the fields during these days. Custom demanded that the bereaved family must not be left alone to brood over their loss. At night they must be helped to keep vigil. For this reason many villagers no longer spent the nights at their homes. The funeral service was held on a Saturday afternoon. It was conducted by a mvangeli of the Methodist Church in front of the main hut. A hymn was sung. A prayer followed. Then another hymn was sung. Some people were called upon to speak and bear witness to the exemplary character of the deceased. The first speaker did not dwell on the circumstances which led to the boy's death. He spoke more about his good home, the earlier years of promise, the cutting off of a young plant before it had matured and had been of service to the community. Another speaker referred to words which had been spoken by the deceased two days before his death, words which now showed that he had known that his death was near. He had thanked his parents for all that they had done for him and had specially asked them not to be discouraged but to show to his younger brothers and sisters the same kindness that they had shown to him. On the eve of his death, it had been reported, Katana had done the unusual thing of praying before he went to bed. It had been given to him to know the day of his death. He had made use of that knowledge and had prepared for that last terrible meeting with his Maker. The Lord gave and the Lord has taken away. Blessed be the name of the Lord. The orator ended his speech on this stirring, dramatic note. The congregation were moved by these revelations. They groaned and made loud exclamations of wonder at the strange and mysterious ways of God.

A third speaker, of the Nkala clan, shook the congregation by making an accusation which afterwards led to the break-up of the Dakada family. He was a fiery, eloquent speaker. He started slowly, apologetically, describing himself as an ungifted speaker who merely blurted out the truth.

'The time has come now for the truth to be spoken,' he said, 'even if the speaker of it stammers. This is a time of death when hidden things must be uncovered and evil exposed. This was a thing done on purpose, this death of Katana. It was deliberate witchcraft, and the wicked woman who did it is known in this village of Kwazidenge. We all know that she has been trying hard, sometimes working through the night, to ruin the Langa family. She has used her daughter to assault a sister of the deceased. She has tried to disgrace the Langa family by telling lies to the police. Now she has used witchcraft to kill Vukubi Langa's son. Some people may blame Zuziwe Langa for Katana's death. That's not true. Zuziwe was only a tool in the hands of the wicked witch of isinga section. Zuziwe did a foolish thing. That can be expected of any girl in love. But why was it Katana, her own brother, who was killed? No. Zuziwe did not cause Katana's death. It's the witch in our midst who did it. And if we wish to avoid the death of others, we must rid ourselves of the witch.'

The speaker had made it obvious to everyone that the witch was Mamtolo, mother of Ntombi. Many villagers received this speech with exclamations and murmurs of anger against the witch that had been denounced. Some said they had known all the time that Mamtolo practised witchcraft. Others asked why it had to be Katana who died. He was not a reckless fighter like Diliza. Mamtolo must have put confusion into his head. She had not even come to the funeral. She knew she was guilty. She must be chased out of Kwazidenge before she killed other people.

Dakada was distressed by the accusation. He sat bewildered after the funeral. The dead boy was forgotten. People discussed Mamtolo and produced more evidence that she was a witch. Who ever heard of a woman taking her daughter to hospital at dead of night after she had been rightly punished by her own father? The woman was up to her evil tricks, that's all. There was no hospital in it. There was nothing wrong with the girl. From the hospital she didn't go to bed as a sick person would do. She went straight to the Charge Office to tell lies, assisted by her demon mother in her evil schemes. Dakada could not deny what the villagers were saying of his wife and daughter. He could not contradict them when they said his wife was a witch. He remembered the evil in his daughter. He had often wondered where she got it from. It could not be from him. Surely he knew himself? His heart was not evil. None of the men of the village had ever accused him of being evil.

If Ntombi did not get her bad heart from him, she must have got it from her mother. So it was possible that she was a witch. But what was he to do? He loved his wife, in a realistic sort of way. She was a hard-working, thrifty woman who looked after him well and made him comfortable. If she was chased away from Kwazidenge, where would he get another woman who would make him and his children comfortable? He did not know.

As Zuziwe was returning home after the funeral, she met Nomi, Zanele and two other girls. She tried to pass them after she had greeted them. But they stopped and forced her to stop and speak to them.

'Have you finished your work, Zuziwe?' asked Zanele.

'What work?'

'Your work of killing Katana?'

'What do you mean?'

'You know very well what I mean,' replied Zanele. 'My words are simple enough. Are you satisfied now that you have killed your brother?'

'It's wicked of you to say that.'

'When will you go to the Thembu village to rejoice with your lover over what you have done?'

'If that's all you wish to say to me,' replied Zuziwe, 'please let me pass.'

They blocked the narrow path. Zuziwe tried to push through the girls. Nomi pushed her back.

'We will let you pass only after we have said all we wish to say to you,' said Zanele. 'I hear the Thembu warrior boys have all been arrested for killing Katana. You too should have been arrested. If you were not such a wicked coward, you would go to the police and surrender yourself and plead for the release of those boys. You enticed that Thembu boy to cross over to you just because you could not control your whorish desire. You ought to be stoned and hounded out of our village. I can't understand why the men are so soft towards you. You must have bewitched them, you witch. How could you sit there quietly while they were accusing mama Dakada of witchcraft when you knew you were the witch? You are evil and cruel. You must have been laughing like a devil in thorough enjoyment of your mischief. It's a pity we are in the village. I'm dying to do to you what Ntombi did at the Xesi river. And I can tell you bhut' Ntabeni won't assault me because of you, as bawo Dakada assaulted Ntombi. Let's go, girls. If I stand here longer, I shall not be able to hold myself off. This girl's fat face is just inviting my fingernails to scratch it.'

Zuziwe sighed with relief when the girls let her by. It was not self-restraint which made them leave her alone. It was the knowledge that there was strength in Zuziwe's apparent weakness. If they attacked her and hurt her, they would be hurt more, as Ntombi had been. They blamed it on the stupidity of men who failed to see the evil in Zuziwe.

Zuziwe was a very unhappy girl. Remorse at the death of Katana tormented her, and yet it was not remorse. Given the same circumstances again, she would act in the same way. She was not ashamed of her pregnancy, but she was anxious about the future. If she could be assured that her future lay with Bhuqa, she would be delighted at the prospect of her coming motherhood. She was more distressed at the breakdown of communication between her and her lover than at the death of her cousin. She could not go to the Thembu village. She dared not go down to the river, either alone, or in the company of others. A feeling of guilt overwhelmed her and prevented her from going anywhere near the scene of that violent encounter under the drooping willow trees. There was just no way of meeting or communicating with Bhuqa. She had been told by one of her sisters-in-law that Bhuqa had been the leader of the Thembu warriors and that he had dealt the blow that had felled Katana, though it was other boys who had finished him off. This, she knew, would complicate the affair still further. She could never hope to win the consent of her parents and relatives to marry Bhuqa.

Waking or sleeping, Zuziwe's mind was in turmoil. In normal times she was not a dreamer when asleep. But after the faction fight she was tormented by nightmares almost every night. She would wake up at dead of night, disturbed by the sheer horror of her dream. One night her sleep was broken by her own shouts and cries. She had been dreaming that she and Bhuqa were walking through a thick forest in which there were wild, fierce beasts. Most of the beasts were strange to her. But she saw a few that she knew. She recognized the vicious leopard, the greedy hyena, the crafty baboon and the stately lion. She remembered afterwards that she was not afraid of the leopard and the lion but became almost sick with fright when either the hyena or the baboon came near her. As they were running away from the beasts, Bhuqa was faster than she was, and he left her behind. She tried to shout, asking him not to leave her behind. But her voice was inadequate and did not seem to reach Bhuqa, for he ran on and did not look back, as if he had forgotten her presence. When she woke up, there were drops of perspiration on her forehead, and her heart was beating like a gong. She was relieved to find that it was a dream, that there were no wild beasts threatening her, and that Bhuqa had not deserted her.

When Dakada went home in the evening, he did not tell his wife at once what the villagers had said. He did not wish to speak about it in the presence of the children. When he and his wife were alone in their hut, he told her briefly what Nkala and the other men had said. Mamtolo flared up at once. She cursed Nkala and analysed him in detail, cutting up his character into small shreds. She was up early in the morning and returned to the subject.

'What does he think he is, that thing with a forehead jutting like a baboon's?' she fumed. 'Has he ever caught me riding a baboon at night? Did you ask him that, Ndlovu?'

'No, mfazi, I didn't ask him.'

'Why didn't you ask him? Go and ask him whether he ever found a witch's broom under the thatch of my hut.'

'It's not Nkala alone who is saying things about you. There are many other people who confirm what he said. I can't challenge all the people of this village and make them shut their mouths.'

The villagers gossiped and tormented Mamtolo. She and Ntombi swore at some women and fought others when they met them in the village. This merely made things worse. They could not fight all the women of Kwazidenge. Dakada decided to take her back to her parents' home at Mnyameni until the trouble ended.

XII | *Court Sequel*

On the night of Katana's death, three Hlubi men had gone to the headman of Kwazidenge to report the boy's death, as was required by law. The headman got up early next day and went to Qoboqobo on horseback, to report the death to the police. Some policemen were despatched from Qonce, a town twenty-six miles away, to reinforce the Qoboqobo police force. A squad of twenty mounted policemen, led by a young officer, left Qoboqobo in the early afternoon of the same day. They urged their powerful horses into a gallop and reached the Thembu village within twenty minutes. They divided themselves into pairs and made a house-to-house search for all boys of the warrior class. They found some of the boys, but others were away. Bhuqa was absent when the officer and his man arrived at his home. The officer was polite but alert. He waited outside whilst his man was searching every hut. He questioned old Ngoma about his son, about the probable time of his return and about his involvement in the faction fight. The old man gave the police officer a full account of the fight, as far as he knew, but withheld two details. He did not reveal the fact that his son had been the leader of the Thembu boys in the fight. Nor did he tell the officer that it was his son who knocked Katana down. Surely, he was not expected to reveal this. It was hearsay. It was for those who saw it with their own eyes to reveal it.

More than half the group of boys who had taken part in the faction fight were arrested. They were brought before the officer, who was waiting near the cattle-kraal of Bhuqa's home. Three of the boys arrested were juniors who had not taken part in the fight. Their parents had protested to the constables who arrested them. The constables had refused to listen to the protests and had rudely told the old people to shut their ugly mouths if they did not wish to get into trouble. They had their instructions, they said. They had to arrest every boy of fighting age. They had to obey the instructions given them by their senior officers. The magistrate would acquit the boys if they were innocent. After questioning the other boys, the officer-in-charge was satisfied that the three juniors had not taken part in the fighting: he released them and warned them to go straight home. They must not warn the boys who had not yet been arrested, or they would find themselves in trouble.

The arrested boys were herded together and driven along the road leading to Qoboqobo like a herd of cattle. They were too many to be handcuffed. Before they left the Thembu village, the officer addressed them and gave them a stern warning not to attempt to escape. The policemen were all armed, he said, and had orders to shoot any boy who attempted to escape. They must all keep together in the middle of the road. The boys did as they were told. They did not wish to give those dangerous-looking policemen a pretext for shooting them down. Two policemen led the group in front, six patrolled each side of the road and four brought up the rear. Two constables were posted at Bhuqa's home, with instructions to arrest Bhuqa and escort him, handcuffed, to the Charge Office. The officer had been informed by some of the constables, who had been told by some of the arrested boys, that Bhuqa had been the leader of the Thembu boys in the faction fight. So he did not want to take any chances. He regarded him as dangerous and wanted to make sure of him.

Bhuqa arrived home late in the afternoon, at the time of day when rabbits begin to come out of their holes. He remained calm when he came upon the two policemen outside the main hut. They explained their business briefly and told him they had orders to arrest him and take him to the Charge Office. The policemen took his stick from him and handcuffed him. They mounted their horses and ordered him to walk briskly beside them.

The other boys had already been locked up in the police cells when Bhuqa arrived at the Charge Office with his police escort. He heard them talking and laughing and shouting, without a care in the world. He was brought before a senior police officer and was instructed to make a statement on the faction fight and the events leading to it. After the statement had been read back to him, he was ordered to sign it. He did all that he was required to do, promptly and willingly. The police officers were impressed by him, by his willingness and intelligence. They locked him up in a cell in which there were only three other Thembu boys. They gave him two more blankets than had been given to the other boys. Bhuqa spent a comfortable night in the cell – as comfortable as it is possible to be in a police cell.

On the following day the rest of the Thembu boys who had taken part in the faction fight were brought to the Charge Office by their fathers. All of them were taken to court and brought before the magistrate, who remanded them for two weeks. They were transferred to the jail at Qonce to await trial. The boys did not seem to care what was done to them, or where they were taken to. They talked and laughed and shouted, unless they were engaged in their favourite mbhayizelo dance. They stamped on the floor of the police truck which transported them to Qonce, and their mbhayizelo grunts were stronger even than the roar of the truck as it struggled uphill on the dusty road leading out of Qoboqobo, or cruised along the neat, black, tarred road leading into Qonce.

The day of the trial came. The small courtroom of Qoboqobo was packed. The accused boys were ushered into the courtroom through a side door. Special seats were arranged for them because there were too many for the usual seats for accused people. Neither could they be made to stand, as was usually done, for then the public at the back of the courtroom would not be able to see the proceedings. The boys filled the courtroom and made it even stuffier. They smiled at friends and relatives in the public seats. Some of the villagers sat on the floor. Others stood leaning against the back wall. Others peeped through the open windows. The prosecutor was a police sergeant, assisted by the officer who had led the arrest of the boys. A constable was having a hard time trying to keep the people quiet and orderly. He had to shout quite often: '*Thulan' enkundleni!* Silence in the court!' even before the magistrate came in. All the people inside the courtroom rose when the magistrate entered.

The case did not last long. No lawyer had been briefed to defend the accused. The charge was read out by the Clerk of the Court. The first accused was Bhuqa, who was asked to plead first. Bhuqa pleaded guilty and all the other boys pleaded guilty after him. The magistrate asked whether any of the accused wished to address the court before he passed sentence. Bhuqa rose and spoke in a strong, clear voice which could be heard inside and outside the courtroom. There was complete silence.

'*Mhlekazi*, your worship, the death of Katana Langa was an accident. It could have been some other Hlubi boy who died on that day. It could have been one of us, Thembu boys. It could have been me. Therefore, I say that it was an accident that it was Katana who was killed. But he knew, when he went down to fight, that he might be killed, as we all knew that we might be killed. It is not in our power to stop these faction fights. They have become a tradition, a way of life of the two villages. If a boy stayed away from a faction fight, he would find that life for him afterwards was worse than death. There is no choice for a boy in this matter, mhlekazi. If you punish us severely today, if you send us to prison, you will be punishing us for something beyond our control. You might as well imprison us because there is drought in the land, or because hundreds and thousands of locusts sweep over the mealie fields and leave destruction and starvation behind, or because a hailstorm beats down the golden tolofiya fruit and the maturing mealie cobs, or because the devil brings down a plague and many people, young and old, fall ill and die. We have as little power to avert a faction fight as we have power to avert these disasters. Impose fines on us. That will be fair enough. We have eaten free food for two weeks. We have enjoyed free trips to Qonce and back. The fines will pay for the food and the trips. Our parents, I am sure, will gladly pay the fines. But do not send us to prison.'

'*Unyanisile, nyana!* You have spoken truly, son!' shouted Bhuqa's father from the back of the courtroom, unable to contain himself. 'Here's the money. We are ready to pay.'

'*Thulan' enkudleni!* Silence in the court!' shouted the police constable.

When the prosecutor was asked to address the court, he said he had nothing to say, except that the state did not oppose the imposition of a fine.

The magistrate sat quietly for some time after the police sergeant had spoken. Then he took his pen and wrote on the sheet of paper spread out on his desk. He raised his head and looked steadily at the crowd of accused boys. The whispering and giggling ceased. But the constable would not be denied the opportunity to assert himself and impress the villagers.

'*Thulan' enkundleni!*' he shouted. It was impossible for the court to be more silent than it had been.

The magistrate spoke. 'The first accused who, I believe, spoke on behalf of all the accused, said many things which, I must admit, are true. I know this district of Qoboqobo well. I agree that faction fights are a regular feature of the life not only of the Thembus and the Hlubis, but also of all the villages in other parts of this district. The village people do not regard a faction fight as an evil thing. Their view of it is the same as that of other people all over the world towards war. It is true that boys have no choice in the matter. They are expected by every man, woman and child in their village to go out and fight.

'But then there is the law of the land to consider. Faction fights are illegal. We must not speak about them in this court as if they are legal. We cannot put them in the same class as the natural phenomena which the first accused listed. There is no law banning plagues, hailstorms, locusts and droughts. These things cannot be said to be illegal, though we all know they are unpleasant and undesirable. But a faction fight is at once unpleasant, undesirable and illegal, and the last of these is the most important aspect for this court. Those who have transgressed the law must be made to feel that they have in fact done so, if the aim of the legislators in making this law is to be realized. They must not be treated as heroes returning from war. A war declared by your country is not illegal. But a faction fight prohibited by the laws of the state is illegal. If the state is not to be undermined, the laws of the state must be upheld. In this case the law allows the court to use its discretion, to impose a fine or a prison sentence. The first accused made a strong appeal for the imposition of a fine instead of a prison sentence. The state does not oppose his plea. But the attitude of every villager towards a faction fight must be corrected. People of every village must be made to feel that faction fights are a danger to the state, that they are a negation of law and order. That is the only way to uproot the tradition, to weed it out and destroy it completely as a way of life of the villages in these parts.

'I find all the accused guilty of culpable homicide as charged. I sentence each of you to two months' imprisonment with hard labour, or a fine of twenty rand.'

The fathers of most of the boys promptly paid the fines and had their sons released. The released boys milled round the courthouse, dancing, and waiting for their comrades' fines to be paid. Bhuqa's father had been the first to pay, and Bhuqa went up and down trying to persuade the men of his village to contribute and help to release all the boys.

Duma and Vukubi Langa watched the triumphant Thembu boys with growing disgust. The boys noted this and deliberately taunted them.

'Kwaaiman!' called out one boy to his friend, using the names used in the boys' world. 'Is the Hlubi dog really dead?'

'Yes, the dog is dead.'

'That surely can't be true. How can we be here, free, and breathing fresh air, if the dog is dead? We ought to be swinging by the neck. I say he's not dead. He just pretended to be dead.'

'I don't know about yours, but my knobkerrie is my witness that the dog is quite dead. It peeped inside the Hlubi skull and gave the Hlubi brains the kiss of death. So the Hlubi dog must be dead.'

'Didn't the magistrate know that our kerries have seen the inside of a Hlubi skull? Why did he free us?'

'Bhuqa's roots were very strong. That's why we are free.'

'Do you think so, Kwaaiman?' asked another boy. 'You

must be right. Bhuqa admitted and we all admitted that we killed the Hlubi boy. And yet, here we are.'

Duma was unable to control himself. He felt he would assault the Thembu boys if he stood there listening to them. He spat on the ground, took Vukubi by the hand and led him away. The boys laughed loud and taunted him further. One of them produced a flute and blew a tune out of it. Others sang: '*Inj' ifile! Inj' ifile!* The dog is dead! The dog is dead!' They all trotted slowly to the rhythm of their song, overtook Duma and Vukubi, greeted them mockingly and passed on to the Thembu village.

And so the Thembu boys returned home in triumph after the court case. Not one of the Thembu people remembered the warning of the magistrate. There was more excitement in the Thembu village on this occasion than on the day when the boys returned victorious from the faction fight. The women ululated, as they always do on important and exciting occasions, adding to the excitement. They ran backwards and forwards, foaming in the mouth, and swept the ground in front of the boys with their shawls. The boys went straight to their favourite spot under the mnquma tree. Here several girls had already gathered to receive them. The girls sang popular songs and the boys danced in circular movements, keeping step. They stamped hard on the ground and reinforced the singing of the girls with the usual mbhayizelo grunts.

Duma's flame of anger set alight the hearts of several other Hlubi people to whom he told the story of the Thembu boys' insulting demonstration of triumph. In this manner the people were prepared for other faction fights in the future. In the evening Duma gave his father and the rest of the family a detailed account of Bhuqa's prominent role at court and after the case.

'Bhuqa has a black heart,' said Duma, looking at Zuziwe. 'It was clear that the court case gave him an opportunity to lead the celebrations today and rejoice publicly over Katana's death, the death of the brother of the girl he is in love with. He addressed the court and boasted that they enjoyed their two weeks' stay in prison where they had plenty of food to eat and free trips to Qonce and back. He saw to it that not one of the Thembu boys was left in jail after the case. He persuaded the Thembu men to pay all the fines. No wonder the Thembu boys were so overjoyed that they composed a song of triumph over our brother's death. That was all Bhuqa's work. I ask you, bawo, to stop Zuziwe from ever again speaking to that boy. She should not be allowed to go to the Thembu village again.'

'I think Zuziwe understands that it will not be wise for her to do so again,' said Mvangeli, looking anxiously at Zuziwe. 'She can see her uncle and aunt when they visit us here.'

This did not satisfy Duma. He wanted his father to give a clear instruction to Zuziwe, forbidding her from meeting or communicating with Bhuqa, and Zuziwe must promise to obey the promise to be made. No one can alter the course of fate. She would do what was reasonable in the circumstances and follow her father's advice and guidance if she was able to do so.

XIII | *The Rivals*

Bhuqa and five other boys of his age-group entered the circumcision school, or went to the forest, as the villagers said, on a very cold morning in the month of May. The bhoma in which they were to live for about three months was hidden from their village but was within easy reach of it. It was at the edge of the wood which lay between the village and the Xesi river. Bhuqa felt quite excited when he approached the bhoma for the first time, because the spot where Zuziwe had accepted his love was only a few yards away. They had spent many sweet hours romancing under the very tree which he could see through the entrance to the bhoma.

Bhuqa wondered whether Zuziwe would visit him during his term in the circumcision school. Girls often visited their lovers when their khankatha was satisfied that the circumcision cuts of all of them had healed. Bhuqa would be delighted if Zuziwe visited him for she was the best of all his girls. Many things had happened since their ill-fated meeting under the willow tree on the banks of the Xesi river. He had got over his unreasonable suspicion of treachery on her part. He longed to look into her eyes, to kiss her, to listen once again to the music of her voice. If she failed to come, well, he had two other girls in the village to entertain him.

He had not ended his affair with them despite his promise to Zuziwe. He had enough time for them. It was not as easy for a girl to leave her home and attend to her love-affairs as it was for a boy.

This put the girls at a disadvantage in their love-affairs. A boy could not be expected to sit alone, unattended, if his partner was unable to leave her home when there was an entertainment. So it had become the accepted practice for each of the bigger boys to have at least two girls. Bhuqa had readily given Zuziwe the promise that he would forgo his former girls because he had been keen that she should accept him. But he had not meant it. After all, he would not see Zuziwe for weeks and weeks. How would he keep himself entertained during those weeks? Zuziwe would not be likely to know that he was still seeing his former girls. If only his sister, Notizi, kept her mouth shut, Zuziwe would not know, and she would not be hurt.

Bhuqa's Thembu girls knew that they were rivals and accepted the position. As long as Bhuqa did not show a preference for one over the other, they were willing to share him. Other girls did the same for less important boys, so why should they not do it for Bhuqa, who was easily the most impressive boy in the village, the leader of the warrior boys? He was handsome. So why should he not have two girls? But they could not bear the thought of sharing him with a third girl, a Hlubi girl, a girl they knew was more beautiful than they were. Their jealousy and hatred of Zuziwe threw them closer together. They met quite often and discussed their common enemy. They went wild with joy when the story reached them that Bhuqa and Zuziwe had received rough treatment under the willows on the banks of the Xesi river.

'Bhuqa must have been quite mad to venture into Hlubi territory for that witch,' said Tozi, one of the girls, when they were together in her room one afternoon a few weeks after Bhuqa had entered the initiation school.

'The girl must have bewitched him,' replied the other girl, named Nozikade. 'He will have to come to his senses now that he has killed his girl's brother. Katana's ghost will not let Katana's own sister sleep with a man who sent him to the land of shadows before his time. She might find that she can't sleep any more if she dares sleep with Bhuqa now. I think events have turned out well for us.'

'When will the khankatha allow us to meet the initiates?' asked Tozi.

'It won't be long now,' replied Nozikade. 'I overheard my father saying that all of them are making good progress and that the cuts are healing well. We will soon hear from Bhuqa. He must send for one of us now that that witch is out of the way.'

'We must punish him a little for neglecting us when that Hlubi girl was here.'

'O yes, let's do so,' Nozikade agreed. 'He must not be allowed to think that he can push us off and pull us back as he likes. He must know what it is to be lonely otherwise he'll never appreciate us. We must not be ever ready to run to him when he nods at us. If we are not careful, the other girls might give us the name they have given to Dabula's girls.'

'What do they call them?'

'They call them "Eveready",' laughed Nozikade.

'Oh, what a name! It serves them right too. They are so conceited. They think so highly of themselves just because they are in love with Dabula.'

'Yes, they think all the other girls would like to be in love with Dabula.'

'Do you know what?' said Tozi. 'When Bhuqa returned from jail, he sent for me twice to meet him in the evening at the edge of the forest. I refused to go. I told him that my father was at home and I couldn't steal out of the house. Of course, I could have gone later in the night when I had finished my work. But I wanted to punish him, to make him feel lonely a bit. I knew you were away from home, visiting your mother's home, and that he had no other girl to go to.'

'You served him well,' said Nozikade. 'I would have done the same too. I can't forget his treatment of us during those two weeks when that rotten girl was here. I agree that we should punish him a little. But we must be careful what we do. We mustn't overdo it.'

'Do you think so?' asked Tozi thoughtfully. 'Perhaps you are right. We mustn't play the fool with him just because we are feeling safe from that Hlubi girl. There may be other girls who want him. Let's not tempt him too much. We must arrange to take turns regularly, to prevent other girls slipping in and robbing us of him as that Hlubi girl did.'

'Yes, I think so,' said Nozikade. 'Besides, their bhoma is in a bad spot. Those trees are quite tempting. I understand it was under those trees that he fell for Zuziwe and they have met there several times.'

Bhuqa and his fellow initiates had been at the circumcision

school for six weeks when their khankatha allowed them more freedom to roam about in the wood and along the bank of the river. But they had to be careful not to be seen by the women of the village. They had to avoid the village and the frequented paths and the river ford. Otherwise, they had complete freedom to meet their girls in the wood or along the riverbank.

During the first week of their freedom, Bhuqa tried to arrange appointments with his Thembu girls, but the appointments failed. He was losing patience. The other initiates returned to the bhoma to boast about their exciting love adventures. One or two stole out in the evening for a late appointment. But this was rare. Their khankatha was accountable to the elders of the village for the safety of the initiates and he always felt more at ease if they were all safe inside the bhoma when he wound his blanket round his body and went home. But from the second week on, Bhuqa's love-affairs righted themselves. His two girls came regularly to see him, taking turns. Bhuqa preferred Nozikade, but he dared not show it. The two girls watched him closely. They had their informants and they seemed to know not only what he did but what he intended doing. So he dared not show his preference for Nozikade.

But Bhuqa yearned for Zuziwe because he loved her best. He had often thought over Zuziwe's wish that they should marry. But marriage seemed to him like a faint light shining dimly and intermittently on the distant horizon. It seemed to be something not quite of this earth. But he could not bear to think of somebody else marrying Zuziwe. That thought made his heart beat like a gong and revived the pain of the healing circumcision cut. He clenched his fists when he thought of that clod, Ntabeni, forcing the girl to marry him. It came out clear in his mind that no one must marry Zuziwe but himself. He could not allow anyone to take her from him. She agreed with his system. There was in her a flavour which he found agreeable to the taste. She was warmer and sweeter than any other girl he had ever kissed and embraced. She seemed to be a part of him, made specially for him. To take her away from him would be like taking away part of his own self. That must never happen.

Now it looked as if his term in the forest would end without a visit from Zuziwe. Notizi tried without success to arrange a meeting between Zuziwe and her brother. She told Bhuqa that Zuziwe's parents would not let her visit the Thembu village again. And on the few occasions when Zuziwe went to the Xesi river, she was always in the company of one or two of her sisters-in-law.

But one day Zuziwe visited Bhuqa. She went down to the Xesi river alone. She left her empty bucket in the care of two little girls near the river, crossed over boldly, walked openly up the slope and went towards the wood where the initiates' bhoma stood. She lingered among the trees near the bhoma until a little boy came out. She sent a message through the boy to Bhuqa and Bhuqa came out. Rumour had reached Zuziwe that Bhuqa met his Thembu girls regularly and that his affair with them had not ended. When they met, Zuziwe was so angry that the words would not come through her lips. Her shapely nose was dotted with drops of perspiration like dew on flower buds. She looked more lovely than ever, with her upper lip pursed and her lower lip pouting like a half-open flower. Bhuqa spoke first.

'Zuziwe, sithandwa, you don't know how delighted I am that you have come here. How did you manage it?'

'That's a lie, Bhuqa,' Zuziwe flung back at him. 'You didn't expect me to come and you didn't want to see me. I know you are well entertained by your Thembu girls. I know that Nozikade and Tozi take turns to visit you and that you embrace them and love them under these very trees where you used to love me.'

'Zuziwe, stop and listen to me,' pleaded Bhuqa.

'I will not listen to you,' replied Zuziwe. 'I have listened to you too much already.'

'You must listen to me, Zuziwe,' said Bhuqa, growing a little angry. 'Someone with mischief in him has lied to you. Whoever he is, he's as clever as the devil. He has mixed truth with lies, his aim being to part us. He knows that those Thembu girls were formerly mine, and that they still claim me and boast that I must give you up and return to them because of the faction fight and the death of your brother. I admit that the girls do come here with the other girls who come to visit their lovers. But I swear to you, Zuziwe, that I stopped being in love with them when I fell in love with you. And that's the whole truth. I plead with you, sithandwa, not to assist the mischief-makers in their mischief. You are my only girl. There can be no other girl for me in the whole of creation.'

Zuziwe did not reply to this eloquent appeal. She did not know whether to believe Bhuqa or not. She felt there was a false note in his voice as he described his love, even though his argument was convincing and his explanation reasonable. It is always difficult for a woman to accept a man's explanation when her jealousy has been roused. Bhuqa suggested that they take a stroll among the trees and talk things over quietly. Zuziwe agreed to this, even though her intuition told her that all was not right. She remained stiff in her manner and guarded in her replies to the questions he asked. But having come so far and at such risk, she could not go back home without enjoying his company, and without one long intoxicating kiss from him. And she would not allow those Thembu girls to triumph over her. So, after a time she thawed down and the two lovers spent a very pleasant afternoon together.

'Bhuqa, I think I'm not well,' Zuziwe told him when they were about to part.

'What's wrong?' asked Bhuqa quietly. 'You look more beautiful than ever. Your cheeks are as rosy as the sun at dawn. You are as inviting and desirable as you have always been.'

'All that is probably because I'm not well,' replied Zuziwe, unsmiling, serious. 'I believe I'm going to have a baby.'

'What! Whose baby? I mean, how do you know you are going to have a baby?'

'Your baby, of course, how can you ask such a question?'

'Forgive me, sithandwa. I didn't mean to ask that. Only I'm surprised. I'm shocked. Are you quite certain you are going to have a baby?'

'I think I'm certain. I have not had my period for two months. Moreover, I can feel there's something inside me. Somehow I feel different, though I can't explain this to you.

But my sisters-in-law seem to be suspicious. They have made comments on my complexion and my breasts and my loss of appetite.'

'I think you should watch yourself for another month or two so as to be quite certain. I shall also try to think out what we should do. My mind is upset now. I don't know what to think.'

Zuziwe agreed to this suggestion and the lovers parted on the banks of the Xesi river.

XIV | *Family Council*

Some weeks after the funeral of Katana Langa, Mvangeli Langa convened a family council to discuss the rupture between Zuziwe and Ntabeni. Several male relatives, Zuziwe's paternal and maternal uncles, and a few other members of the Bhele clan, responded to his call. The first man to arrive was Vukubi Langa. He came at noon on the appointed day. Others came later in the afternoon. The shadows of the trees were beginning to lengthen when it was felt that the meeting should begin. The men, eight in number, met in the dining-room, and the women prepared food in the kitchen and on the fireplace outside. Mvangeli addressed the assembled men.

'MaBhele, I have called you here as the fathers of this home to decide on a matter which concerns your daughter, Zuziwe, and Ntabeni, her fiancé. Zuziwe has rejected him. She wrote to him and told him so. Ntabeni appealed to me. He refused to accept Zuziwe's rejection of him.'

'What did you say to Ntabeni when he came to you?' asked one bawokazi.

'I told him I could not compel Zuziwe to marry him against her will. They must make it up between them.'

'You have already given your decision on this matter. What do you now require of us?' asked a second bawokazi.

'Ntabeni came to ask me to try to persuade Zuziwe to take him back. I refused to do that. That's all I did. But she's your child. You have to decide what to do now.'

'Mkhuluwa is quite right,' said a third bawokazi. 'The choice is ours whether to compel Zuziwe to marry Ntabeni or to allow her to reject him. Speaking for myself I don't think it wise to compel the girl to marry a man she doesn't like.'

'She liked him once,' exclaimed the first bawokazi angrily. 'What has changed her love to hatred? Is it because of something she has discovered in him or because she has seen some other young man? We can't allow her to change lovers as if they were frocks.'

'Is there any truth in the rumour that Zuziwe is in love with a Thembu boy?' asked a Bhele of the surname of Khubalo.

As no one ventured to answer this question, it was decided that Zuziwe be called in. She came in after a delay of some minutes. She knew that hard words would be spoken to her, that a girl was never called in to a family council of male relatives except to be bullied and insulted. She knew also that the assembled men were not likely to promote the interests of the child in her womb and of the father and mother of the child. For these reasons she was not eager to obey the summons. When she entered the room, she was received in complete silence. A grunt from one bawokazi was the only reply she received to the greeting she gave as she stood hesitating before the grey-bearded men. She sat on a grass mat spread on one side of the room, close to the wall, behind some of the men who were sitting on low stools.

'Find yourself a stool and sit here in front of us,' said the first bawokazi in a gruff voice. 'Why do you hide yourself?'

Zuziwe went to the kitchen and brought back with her an empty paraffin tin to sit on.

The first bawokazi spoke again. 'Zuziwe!'

'Bawokazi.'

'Is it true that you have rejected Ntabeni?'

'It is true, bawokazi.'

'Are you so daring as to break down a house which we, your fathers, are trying to build? Are you driving us away from this home of ours?'

'No, bawokazi, I'm not driving you away.'

'If you break down a house that we are building, then you are driving us away. You are lowering us in the eyes of the villagers. We shall not come here to manage the affairs of this home if you do this. Understand this clearly, girl. Reject Ntabeni and you reject us. If you reject us, a flood of water enters the house, as we say. Disaster will be your lot. You will become an outcast, a thing with no law, with no authority, with no order. If you marry Ntabeni, you are on the side of law and order. You will be striking a blow against all enemies of order and decency, against the devil, against sin itself. My child, listen to me. I'm much older than you are. I know what I'm speaking about. A house built by your fathers is built on rock. It will not fall. Do not be blinded by love. Love is air. You cannot build a house on it. If there's a boy whose sweet words have beguiled you, turn your back on him. If he has the heart to persuade you to act against your parents, he is a bad man. Cut all ties that bind you to him. Rip him out of your system. Bear the pain of giving him up now rather than suffer the endless agony of living in hell with him for the rest of your life. He is the devil's own son. He's not a young man fit for a decent girl to marry. I have spoken. I shall not speak again on this matter.'

Zuziwe was surprised. The old man did not speak in the usual bullying tone of a bawokazi intimidating his niece, except at the beginning of his speech. He was appealing to her better judgement. The other men were perplexed. The meeting had taken an unusual turn. It was left to Zuziwe's father to speak next.

'Ntombi yam, Zuziwe, your bawokazi is appealing to you to think clearly in this matter. Ntabeni is known by all of us in this village to be an industrious, steady, reliable man, whatever his faults may be. And who of us is without faults, my child? You can build a home for your children with such a man. A man you know is to be preferred to a strange man, to a man who comes from a hostile village, who has been taught to hate and destroy your people. Do not hide from your fathers the fact that there's an understanding between you and that Thembu boy who led the attack against our boys, who struck the blow that killed our son. The truth is known all over Kwazidenge. But how can he truly love you? Ask yourself that question. Deep down in his heart, perhaps unknown even to himself, there must be some lingering hatred of you. This hatred will erupt one day and destroy you and your children and all you hold dear in the world. Let us advise you in this affair. You are young, very young. You have no experience of life. There's a heap of tomorrows ahead of you. Be careful how you prepare for those tomorrows. Take the man whom your fathers have chosen, and your future will be as bright as sunshine. But if you take the man who has dazzled you, whose circumstances are so unfavourable to yours, then your future will be as dark as the clouds before a thunderstorm.'

Her father's words, coming so close upon the words of the first bawokazi, were too much for Zuziwe to bear. She burst into tears and cried hysterically. Her mother came in and led her out of the room.

'What's wrong with this girl?' asked Khubalo heatedly. 'Is she bewitched? Why does she cry? The fault is in you, maBhele. You are too gentle with her.'

'Khubalo is right,' agreed Vukubi. 'You ought to tell the girl what to do. Why do you plead with her like a young, green lover pleading for a girl's love? If she refuses to obey, then let us knock sense into her head. She must purge herself of that bloodthirsty Thembu boy and marry Ntabeni.'

'And yet,' said Mvangeli softly, 'in these affairs of the heart, if the girl is persuaded instead of compelled, it is better by far. Much trouble and suffering may be caused if force is used. It was for this reason I told Ntabeni the two of them must settle this matter themselves.'

'Where then do we come in, if that's the case?' asked Khubalo angrily. 'What part do we play?'

'We have a very big part to play,' replied Mvangeli. 'These children cannot be lawfully united, nor can their union be blessed, if we do not play our part.'

'We can't allow ourselves to be led by the nose by a girl. We arrange this affair as we see fit or she marries herself to this Thembu ruffian like the lawless hussy that she is.'

The first bawokazi had remained quiet as he had said he would, after his strong appeal to Zuziwe. But now Mvangeli appealed to him to say the last word.

'We do not know what Zuziwe is thinking,' he said, after a brief silence. 'She has not told us of any Thembu boy who has promised to marry her. It's clear that there's a conflict in her mind and that she has not taken a decision. Perhaps she doesn't mean to marry this boy. The very fact that she has not told us about him when she had the chance to do so makes me feel that there is yet hope. Perhaps our gentle words of appeal will help her to take the right decision. She's probably calmer now and can tell us her real feelings. I suggest that her father and mother speak to her alone in her bedroom.'

This suggestion was grudgingly agreed to by the Bhele council. Mvangeli went out to speak to Zuziwe. But when he entered the bedroom he found that there was no need for him or his wife to try to persuade her. He was much surprised when his wife told him that Zuziwe was quite willing to marry Ntabeni.

'Do you understand clearly what this means, Zuziwe?'

'Yes, tata, I do.'

'Have you decided to give up the Thembu boy and marry Ntabeni at once?'

'Yes, tata, I have.' She was scarcely audible.

'Do you give me your solemn promise that you will have nothing to do with that Thembu boy in future?'

Instead of answering this question, Zuziwe burst into violent, uncontrollable, frame-rocking sobs.

'Please leave her alone, father of Zuziwe,' said Mrs Langa.

'You are hurting her. There's a mystery here. There must be something troubling her. Perhaps her decision to give up Bhuqa has hurt her deeply.'

Mvangeli left the room without saying another word. He returned to the council and gave his report, which was received with grunts of approval by most of them. The first bawokazi did not comment, but his face wore an expression which clearly said, 'I thought so.'

One or two women came in with dishes of food, a mixture of samp and beans, flavoured with gravy and crowned with a chunk of meat. This was their favourite food. So they got down to it and enjoyed it to the full. They twitted the women who were moving in and out, attending to them. The hot afternoon changed into cool evening and they decided it was time to go back home.

Khubalo did not go straight home. He decided to go and congratulate Ntabeni for his perseverance and for winning Zuziwe after all the trouble she had given him. Ntabeni did not believe what Khubalo told him.

'I'm telling you the truth, Thole,' said Khubalo. 'That Bhele girl will marry you as soon as you have paid all the lobola cattle demanded. I've just come from a meeting of the Bhele clan. Several things were cleared up at that meeting. The girl is ready to marry you. You should never have doubted it. We Bhele men don't allow a daughter of ours to bully us in a matter of marriage.'

'It's her father who discouraged me. He spoils his daughter. He is weak. He told me he would not compel the girl to marry me.'

'Yes, I know. My brother is altogether too soft with

Zuziwe. You'll have to deal firmly with her if you hope to have peace of mind when she's your wife.'

'You know me well, Bhele,' said Ntabeni, his eyes glowing with a sense of his own importance. 'I have no time for nonsense.'

After this visit Ntabeni became a happy, confident man again. The sanuse's philtre must have produced some effect in some mysterious way after all, he thought, even though he had failed to serve it on Zuziwe. Perhaps the very possession of it with the girl continually in his mind drew her to him. He seemed to expand, and he made his presence felt as he moved about in the village. He spoke loudly and laughed heartily in the knowledge that he would soon marry the most beautiful girl in Kwazidenge. But alas, before many weeks had passed, several things happened which made him shrink again.

XV | *Unborn Baby*

Why did Zuziwe suddenly yield? Why did she agree to marry Ntabeni whom she had grown to hate worse than anybody else in Kwazidenge? The reason was her pregnancy. She had told no one at home about it. She had come to the realization that Bhuqa was unable to marry her. She had at last understood that there were too many obstacles in the way. Some weeks before, she had again gone to the woodland near the Thembu village and had sent for Bhuqa, who had left the initiation school. Bhuqa was at home and he went to her at once.

'Zuziwe, why do you come here without an appointment?' he asked in a trembling voice. 'Why have you sent for me so urgently? It was fortunate your message came when I was at home.'

'If you don't make an effort to meet me, I must force my way to you,' replied Zuziwe, her eyes filmy with tears. 'I've written twice to you, asking you what you've decided to do. You haven't cared to reply or even to indicate that you received my letters. I met Notizi at the ford last week and asked her to give you a message from me. That produced nothing. It became clear to me that I must seek you out, at your home if necessary. I'm carrying your child in me and I want to know what you intend doing about it.'

'I haven't deserted you, Zuziwe. I've been having trouble at home ever since I told my father about you after my return from the initiation school. He will not allow me to marry you.'

'Why don't you tell him that you've made me jilt a man who had promised to marry me and that you have made me pregnant?'

'I've told him all that. But his heart is hardened against you and all your people. I didn't know that he hated your people so much. I fought against Hlubi boys because it was expected of me and because of the excitement it gave me, not out of hatred. But my father hates you and your people with every drop of blood in his body. He was shocked to hear that I love you, a Hlubi girl, and that I wish to marry you. I asked some of my relatives to help me. A few of them sympathized with me and tried to speak to him. But my father became very angry and threatened to throw them out of his house. My other relatives supported my father in his decision.'

'Why do you tell me all this, Bhuqa? What have I to do with your relatives? They didn't make me pregnant. They are not responsible for the child in me. You are. If your relatives don't care for me, then I don't care for them too. You are not a child. You can't be made by other men to neglect your clear duty. You have not yet told me what you intend doing.'

'Zuziwe, there are only two courses open to us. And neither of them is easy. We could marry secretly, and then you could go with me to Port Elizabeth, where I shall soon be taking up a job in the police force. We could share a two-roomed house with a friend of mine who works in Port Elizabeth. Or you could go alone to my aunt who lives at Mathole village, ten miles from here. But she's very poor. She lost her husband two years ago. She has to do the washing of a family living on a farm near by. She's paid very little for it. If you go there, I shall have to feed you together with my aunt and her children.'

'How can I live with your aunt, Bhuqa, if your father doesn't want me to be your wife? He will compel your aunt to throw me out as soon as he learns that I'm living with her.'

'You'll have to go with me to Port Elizabeth, though we shall be quite a crowd for a two-roomed house.'

'Is your friend married?'

'Yes, he's married and they have one child.'

'How could two families live in a two-roomed house, Bhuqa? If there had been two bedrooms and a kitchen, it would be possible. Will your friend welcome you together with a wife? Does he know you will bring a wife with you?'

'No, he doesn't. I didn't know it myself until now. I'm just trying to work out a plan. But I know he'll welcome me. We are old friends. I know he would rather go out and live elsewhere to make room for me than see me stranded in a strange city.'

'Do you know his wife? Will she agree to the arrangement? The man may be willing to share his house with you. But women are not like men in such matters. You'd better write to your friend before you decide what to do.'

Bhuqa followed Zuziwe's advice and wrote. The reply proved Zuziwe right. Bhuqa's friend would have been quite willing to receive them into his house, he said, if his mother-in-law had not been living with them. But now his mother-in-law slept in the kitchen with children of relatives, and he slept in the bedroom with his wife and his small child. Bhuqa's friend added that it would be unlikely that Bhuqa's wife would be permitted to live in Port Elizabeth. Influx control laws were very rigid. Men who were permitted to enter the urban area of Port Elizabeth were given single accommodation in hostels. They were not allowed to bring their families with them. Bhuqa decided to leave for Port Elizabeth at once to see things for himself. He was confident that a solution could be found. Things could not be as bad as his friend said. He would return in a few months, he told Zuziwe, marry her secretly and take her to Port Elizabeth with him.

After a few weeks Bhuqa realized that it was impossible to get a permit for Zuziwe, whom he represented as his wife, to enter Port Elizabeth. There were many people, men and women, who were being endorsed out of Port Elizabeth for one reason or another, though they had lived there for many years. They were replaced by migratory labourers, men who signed contracts to work for a fixed period of six months or nine months or a year, after which they had to return to their rural villages, even if their firm or factory still had work for them. They lived in hostels. Their wives were not allowed to enter the urban area. Bhuqa wrote to Zuziwe and told her what the position was. She would have to go and live with his aunt at Mathole.

This, then, was the state of affairs when Zuziwe told her parents on the day of the family meeting that she was willing to marry Ntabeni. The ache in her heart was unbearable. It was clear to her that Bhuqa could not marry her for the simple reason that he had nowhere in the world to take her. With Bhuqa disowned by his father, as he would be if he married her, and with Zuziwe shut out of all urban areas by influx control laws, Bhuqa would not be able to provide a house for her to live in. Nor could he obtain a hut or a site at another rural village. There were influx control laws of a sort even there. Sites, he was told by one of the headmen to whom he applied, were scarce enough for their own children, children of the soil. He, the headman, would be torn to pieces by the villagers if he allotted a site to a stranger. Bhuqa was advised to make it up with his father and return to the village where he belonged.

Zuziwe had to suffer a double loss. She had to lose the man she loved and the baby growing up quietly in her womb. Her decision to give up Bhuqa and marry Ntabeni was at the same time a decision to sacrifice her unborn baby by committing abortion. Young as she was, she had to take this decision alone. After she had taken it, after she had told her parents that she had made up her mind to marry Ntabeni, she recoiled from the act. She thought of committing suicide by taking poison or by letting a snake bite her in the woods or by falling over the cliffs overlooking the Xesi river, or by accepting the call of the people of the river by drowning herself in its deep waters. Perhaps she would be happier in another world. She, like all other children of Kwazidenge, had always feared the people of the river. It was common practice for children to stand on the riverbank and shout hard to warn the people off before jumping in to swim. But now she felt that the world of the people of the river could not be half as bad and cruel as her own. She had never seen them come out to fight among themselves or against the people of the earth. Or was it mere superstition that there were people in the river?

But how could she go on living after giving up the man she loved and destroying his child? Why should she love so much the man she ought to hate? Why were the Thembus and the Hlubis such resolute enemies? The individuals were ordinary, decent, normal people with normal feelings and desires. It was the group feeling, the group hatred, which turned them into angry, unforgiving maniacs. In their madness they made a virtue of a vice. Was it part of the irony of life that she should be compelled to turn away from the man she loved, the man who loved her, and embrace a man she did not love; that she should be compelled to raise her hand against her unborn baby lying, trustingly, in the innermost recesses of her body? What cruel justice was this that was meted out to her, to her lover, to her innocent baby? Must she defy the world and give birth to her illegitimate child, and allow it to face the taunts and jibes of a cruel world? No, she could not bear that. Must she then destroy her own child, the flesh of her own flesh, she, who ought to protect it and defend it to her last breath? No, she could not do that either. No! Again and again, no! But what must she do? She must go to her aunt at the Thembu village, lay bare her heart to her and follow her advice. She had thought she had come to a firm decision when she told her parents she would marry Ntabeni. But now she did not know what to do.

On the day after the family meeting, Zuziwe took some money which Bhuqa had sent her. She told her mother she intended spending a few days with her uncle and aunt at the Thembu village. As it was known that Bhuqa was away from home, her parents did not object. They felt that a change of air would be good for her. She was very fond of her uncle and aunt and their home was almost like a second home. Zuziwe told her aunt the full story of her love, its joys and sorrows, and the disastrous way in which it was likely to end. Her aunt knew the greater part of the story, but she had not known the fearful conflict in which her niece found herself. She too found it difficult to decide.

'Are you quite sure that Bhuqa cannot get you a permit to live with him in Port Elizabeth? Is there no way at all?'

'That's what he says, Auntie,' replied Zuziwe, 'and I do believe he has tried hard to get it.'

'Has he thought of offering money to an official to help him out? I've heard that many people got theirs that way.'

'Yes, he has. But as a policeman, he has to be very careful. In his letter he told me some officials had been arrested, charged and convicted a short while ago for accepting bribes and forging permits. None of the officials are willing to help now. Besides, some of his friends told him he must be particularly careful when making an offer of money. Some officials accept money and pretend to be doing something even when they are doing absolutely nothing. You lose all the money you have paid and it's usually a lot. No, if I went to Port Elizabeth I would have to go without a permit and live the life of a fugitive. I don't wish to do that. If I got caught, Bhuqa might find himself in trouble. If he lost his job in the police force and was endorsed out of Port Elizabeth, where would we go?'

'No, that wouldn't do,' agreed her aunt. 'But I'm against abortion. It's a dangerous thing and it's a sin against God who alone gives life. You would be turning God's blessing into a curse if you got rid of your unborn baby. Let your baby come. Your father will be terribly disappointed in you but he'll not chase you away from home. If he did so at first, you could come and live with us. We shall always be ready to receive you, whatever your misfortune.'

'But Auntie, when I told my parents that I was ready to marry Ntabeni, it was because I had decided to commit abortion first and then submit myself to the will of my parents and relatives and accept my cross. How can I take back what I have said? I cannot marry Ntabeni when I know I'm carrying another man's child.'

'You must tell your parents everything and leave it to them to decide what to do. Put your trust in them. They will do the best for you in the circumstances. Without their help and without Bhuqa's help you will make things worse than they are.'

'Is there any hope, do you think, that Bhuqa will one day marry me and take me away to some far away place where there are no enemies, no hatred, no influx control, where he could live happily with me and my child?'

'There's no place like that, child. Don't trust Bhuqa too much. His behaviour in this affair has not been quite right. And he's not as reliable as you think. I've had to speak strongly to him about his continued love-affairs with other girls in this village after getting involved with you. I've always avoided speaking to you about this because I was afraid of hurting you. I was hoping he would reform. Now I must say he has disappointed me. His father has been urging him to marry Nozikade, whom he has been seeing for a long time, and I learn he's not strongly opposed to this. Perhaps this is one of the reasons why he has not asserted himself and insisted on marrying you, whatever the consequences, as a man of resolution should have done.'

When her aunt spoke of Bhuqa's weakness of character, his lack of firmness, his infidelity, Zuziwe turned her face away and looked through the open window at the distant Bhukazana peak, which was covered with snow, and at the afternoon sky, which was slowly becoming overcast. She looked at these objects with fixed, unseeing eyes. She stared at the darkening view. She continued to breathe, and her blood continued to flow. But the rose in her cheeks faded and the sparkle in her eyes died out. She gave the impression of a lifeless statue. Her aunt was shocked at her numbness. She tried to revive the girl's spirits, to assure her that all would end well, though she could not say how. She thought it would help if they returned to the hut which was used as a living-room and re-joined the rest of the family. But Zuziwe preferred to go to the hut which was reserved for her. There she undressed and went to bed without waiting for supper.

She got up early next day and told her uncle and aunt that she was returning home. They were both surprised and disappointed that she was cutting short her visit. They tried to persuade her to stay a few days longer. Zuziwe thanked them for the kindness and love with which they had always treated her, but she refused, quietly and firmly, to stay longer with them.

Notizi took Zuziwe as far as the river ford. Zuziwe pretended to return home, but as soon as Notizi disappeared round a bend, she turned round and followed a path leading to Qoboqobo. She walked briskly. It was early and there were very few people on the road. On her arrival in town, she went to the house of a midwife who had a lucrative private practice. This midwife helped to deliver the babies of women who did not wish to go to Mthwaku Hospital for confinement. She charged a moderate fee for her services. She visited her patients both before and after confinement. She was efficient. Her office was well equipped, and she gave good professional attention to her patients. Despite all this, many families preferred the old, untrained village midwives for whom no fee was paid. The professional midwife would have found things difficult, had she not supplemented her lawful practice with another not so lawful. She helped many unmarried expectant mothers to get rid of their unwanted babies. For these services her fees were high, but she had a thriving business. Her patients came from far and near, and from all classes of people. An occasional generous gift to the officer commanding the local police station helped to keep her out of legal trouble.

Zuziwe was given quick, expert attention, after she had explained briefly that she was a few months pregnant, and that she wanted to get rid of the baby. The operation did not last long, nor did it give her much pain. She went back home hardly believing that the midwife had done what she wanted her to do. She arrived home at midday and made herself some coffee. She moved in and out of the house, helping her mother and her sisters-in-law to do the housework. Sometimes she hoped that the operation had served its purpose and that her problems were about to be solved by the abandonment of her dearest wishes and the sacrifice of herself to Ntabeni. At other times she prayed that it would fail and that she would give birth to her baby. In the late afternoon she began to bleed a little. As the afternoon grew into evening and evening grew into night, she bled so much that her mother noticed that there was something wrong. Mother Langa came into Zuziwe's bedroom and found Zuziwe lying under a blanket on her bed, with some of her underwear hanging on the bed railings.

'Zuziwe, my child, what's wrong? Your underwear is full of blood. What makes you bleed so much? Are you ill?'

'No, mama, I'm not ill. I'm having my period. Only I'm bleeding more than usual this time.'

'We must send at once for the doctor, for Dr Sango. This bleeding looks quite serious.'

'No, mama, don't send for the doctor. I'll be all right. The bleeding will soon stop.'

'When did you start bleeding?'

'This afternoon, mama.'

'Has it stopped now? What are you using to prevent the blood from spoiling the sheets?'

'I'm using pads in the usual way. And I've spread an old blanket on the sheet.'

Mrs Langa insisted that Zuziwe remove the blanket so that she might satisfy herself about the condition of the sheet and the mattress. She was shocked to see the pool of blood in which her daughter was lying.

'Zuziwe, my child, what's this?' she asked anxiously. 'What's happening to you? Tell me everything. I'm your mother. I can't help you if I don't know what has gone wrong. Are you having an abortion?'

'Yes, mama.'

'Who made you pregnant? Is it Bhuqa?'

'Yes, mama.'

Mrs Langa went out quickly. She found her husband reading his Bble in the dining-room. She called him into their bedroom and told him what was happening. She cut short his exclamations, saying it was no time for anger but for quick action if their daughter was to be saved. She could die from loss of blood alone, if the actual abortion did not kill her. He must send at once for Dr Sango. The old man hurried out and went to Duma's hut. He told Duma to saddle his horse and ride as fast as he could and fetch Dr Sango. It was fortunate that Duma was at home. He liked to visit his neighbours and pass the earlier part of the night in a quiet chat with them over a pipe. But tonight he was at home. It was fortunate also that his horse, which was usually knee-haltered and allowed to wander over the veld, was tethered to the old tree near the cattle-kraal.

Dr Sango was about to go to bed when Duma came and explained his sister's trouble to him. He told Duma to tether his horse to a fence post and come with him in his car. He drove speedily to the Langa home. The young doctor worked for two hours, trying all he knew to stop the bleeding. But Zuziwe bled on. She was becoming weaker and weaker through loss of blood. Dr Sango advised that she be taken at once to Mthwaku Hospital if she was to be saved. He offered to take her in his car. Mama Langa must come along with her. When Zuziwe was told to rise from her bed and prepare for a trip to the hospital, she refused to move. She shook her head slightly and made no move to rise.

'No, mama,' she said, 'it's not necessary for me to go to Mthwaku Hospital. I want to die. I myself alone decided to destroy my baby. It will be a blessing to me to die with my unborn baby. It will save me much suffering. It will be one of the best things that God has done for me. Don't take away my blessing from me. Thank you, Dr Sango, for your kindness. But there's very little you can do for me. It's no use trying to save my body when you cannot save my soul from the fate that has been fixed for it. I have lost my lover. I have destroyed my own baby. I cannot marry the man whom you, my parents, were urging me to marry because the abortion which I have tried to keep secret will be made known to the world when I am admitted at Mthwaku Hospital. Then why should I, who have lost all, desire to live? No, mama. Please, tata, if you love me, if you feel for me in this, let me lie here on this bed and bleed slowly to death.'

'Zuziwe, my baby,' replied Mrs Langa, with tears streaming down her cheeks, 'do not ask me to stand at your bedside and see you bleed to death. How can I, who bore the pangs of birth for you, stand by and see you die? Do not ask it of me, child, you with whom I sealed my womb when I got you. My own life would become meaningless after your death. After such a death. Help us, my child, allow us to do all we can to save you. Let the good doctor take you in his car to Mthwaku Hospital.'

'Your mother is right, Zuziwe,' said old Langa, speaking in a hoarse voice, his eyes filled with tears of grief, for Zuziwe was his favourite child, the child of his old age. 'You are not going to die. It is God alone who decides the day of your death, not you yourself. It is an evil thing to try to force God's hand. He has sent Dr Sango to come and help you. Rise from your bed, Zuziwe, my child, and let us do what we can to save you.'

'As you please, tata. If it will give you peace of mind, I consent to be taken to Mthwaku. But I tell you it's useless. Neither you nor Dr Sango nor all the learned doctors at Mthwaku Hospital can thwart the will of the unseen power that is pressing me towards my doom. I'm ready, doctor. Come, mama, let's go. It grows late. There's no time.'

They arrived at Mthwaku Hospital at three o'clock in the morning. Zuziwe was admitted at once. But she was not operated upon until nine o'clock, and she had bled all the time. The operation was successful as far as it went. The aborted baby was removed and the womb scraped clean. But Zuziwe continued to bleed. A team of doctors and staff nurses worked on her for two hours, trying in vain to stop the flow of blood. Her heart beat more and more slowly, and at one o'clock in the afternoon it stopped, and all the earthly troubles of Zuziwe Langa ended.

XVI | *Funeral Again*

The Hlubi village was stunned by the death of Zuziwe. Some people condemned her for the crime of abortion, by which she had tried to conceal her sin. Her parents were grieved not only by her death but also by the village gossip which followed.

Mrs Dakada heard of Zuziwe's death and the details of it at Qoboqobo, where she had gone to meet her husband. 'Do you see now, Ndlovu,' she asked, 'do you see that Ntombi was right in what she said about this girl, and that you were wrong in taking her side?'

'I didn't take her side,' replied Dakada. 'I objected to Ntombi's assault on the girl. If Zuziwe was unfaithful, Ntabeni should have dealt with her, not Ntombi.'

'Do you still doubt it? Why do you say "if"? Of course she was unfaithful. Her pregnancy has made that quite clear. This girl must have bewitched you, I think. She was the witch of Kwazidenge. Perhaps you were her secret lover. You must have urged Nkala to accuse me of witchcraft so that you might get rid of me. I wondered why you refused to fight Nkala for telling lies about me in public. Now it's as clear as the lake on the summit of Bhukazana mountain. You wanted to be free to go and sleep with that whore. Fortunately for me the Thembu boy got in first. And more fortunately still, she's dead now, unless you want to go and make love to her corpse, the corpse of a witch, a whore, a murderer. You ought to hang your head with shame, Ndlovu. How could you, a white-haired old man, feel passion for such a young girl? Did you really have the desire in your blood for that child? Sies! You are a dirty old man.'

'Did you ask me to come and meet you here so that you could swear at me?' asked Dakada, his upper lip trembling with anger. 'If that is all you want to do, then I'm going back to Kwazidenge. You can go back to Mnyameni and stay there until your mother teaches you how to speak to your husband.'

With these words Dakada turned his back on Mamtolo, went to his horse, jumped on its back and rode off. Fortunately for Mamtolo, her husband had already ordered the shopkeeper, who knew them to be good customers, to supply her with the groceries she needed. She explained to him that her husband had suddenly gone home and had forgotten to leave money behind. The shopkeeper agreed to supply her with the goods as he was confident that Dakada would pay for them next time he came to town.

Bhuqa took a week's leave and returned home when the news of Zuziwe's death reached him. He felt he was unable to fix his mind on his work. He therefore decided that he must go and re-visit those places which for him had close associations with Zuziwe: the Xesi river, whose waters were at this time as clear and as full of laughter as her eyes; the woodland where he had passed some of the sweetest hours of his young life with her. The passing of Zuziwe seemed to have cleared the mist of confusion in his mind.

But in his heart there remained an ache as sharp as the prick of a knife. He wished to attend her funeral, to look at her lovely face for the last time as it lay in its final resting place. But he did not know whether he would be allowed to do this.

Soon after his arrival at home, Bhuqa visited Zuziwe's uncle and aunt. They had just returned from Kwazidenge when he went to them. The grief on their faces drew a tear or two from his eyes. Zuziwe's aunt did not wish to speak to Bhuqa. She left the two men alone and withdrew to the hut which Zuziwe had always used as her bedroom. The men spoke for some time about Bhuqa's work as a policeman and his experiences at Port Elizabeth. Then Bhuqa spoke about the funeral. When he spoke Zuziwe's name, his heart danced inside his ribs.

'When will Zuziwe be buried, bawo?' he asked.

'Tomorrow,' replied the other man.

'Do you think it will be in order if I attend the funeral?' asked Bhuqa, slowly, hesitantly.

'Yes, I think so, nyana. My brother-in-law is a good man. He is a true man of God. He will not object to your presence. It's his sons that I'm not so sure of, and the other Bheles. But if you arrive just in time for the service at midday, and leave immediately after the funeral, there'll be no trouble. They wouldn't dare chase you away from the funeral service. Do you really wish to go to this funeral?'

'Yes, bawo, I do.'

'Why? I was told you had given up Zuziwe and decided to marry Nozikade.'

'No, bawo, that was not my decision. That was my father's

decision. Zuziwe died because my father didn't want her, not because I didn't want her. My father hates her people. He wanted me to hate them too. He threatened to throw me out of the house if I married a Hlubi girl. I tried to make him understand that I was not asking to marry a Hlubi girl. I wished to marry a girl called Zuziwe Langa whose heart was as beautiful as her face. I wish to God there were no such things as Hlubis or Thembus and that there were only people. Had it been so, I wouldn't have lost my Zuziwe.'

'I don't understand, nyana. Were you not making arrangements to marry Nozikade? Is there no truth in the story that Zuziwe got rid of your child because you disappointed her?'

'The story is both true and untrue, bawo,' replied Bhuqa, his eyes fixed on the floor.

'What do you mean? Is this a jest or a riddle?'

'It's true that Zuziwe got an abortion because I disappointed her. But it's not true that I am making arrangements to marry Nozikade. My father is making the arrangements. And if he continues, he'll have to marry her himself. My wife is lying dead at Kwazidenge and I shall attend her funeral tomorrow. If her brothers want to kill me and help me to join her where she is, I am ready to accept that as my fate. I am not pretending that I want to die. No. I don't want to die. I'm young. Perhaps I shall find another girl whom I shall love as well as I loved Zuziwe. And I pray that when I find her, I shall not be dependent upon my father for a place to live in. I shall not allow him to force his will upon me again.'

On the following day, a little before midday, Bhuqa went to Zuziwe's funeral. He crossed the Xesi river without trouble. The stepping stones showed high above the water. He remembered the stone which had failed him when he tried to help Zuziwe cross over. He still felt a pang of regret at his failure to help her. He walked steadily towards Kwazidenge. He was about to enter the village when he met Mlenzana, who was also on his way to the funeral. Bhuqa was pleased to see him. He had not seen Mlenzana since the day of the faction fight. Mlenzana had gone to the initiation school with other Hlubi boys of his age at the same time as Bhuqa. It was fortunate for Bhuqa that it was Mlenzana whom he met at this particular moment, because Mlenzana was one of the few people in Kwazidenge, apart from Mvangeli's own family, who fully understood why Zuziwe died. With a depth of penetration beyond his years, he saw Zuziwe as a victim of prejudice and hatred. He hoped her blood was not spilt in vain and that it would help put out the angry fire in the villagers' hearts. He hoped they would learn to value a man as a human being, and not hate him just because he came from the other village.

Mlenzana's influence grew as he grew older. He became accepted as the leading spirit of the youth of the day. Other young men listened to him respectfully when he spoke against faction fights because they knew it was not cowardice but conviction which made him condemn the fights. They remembered that in the actual fight he was as brave as the bravest of them. They did not agree with him, but one or two felt that there was some truth in what he said.

Bhuqa and Mlenzana went along together to the home of the Langas, talking sadly of the tragedy which had befallen not only the Langa family, not only the village of Kwazidenge, but all people of goodwill everywhere.

Some people saw them as they approached and thought it strange that these two young men should come to the funeral together. It appeared strange to them because one of them was a Thembu, guilty of spilling the blood of a Langa young man, and guilty also of the death of Zuziwe to whose funeral he had come.

'Why is that villain attending the girl's funeral?' It was Ntabeni who asked this question, edging away from the spot where the two young men had seated themselves. It was disgust, not fear, which made Ntabeni edge away from Bhuqa.

Duma heard the question and looked up from the paper on which he was recording money contributions from the mourners. He froze when he saw Bhuqa. Then he boiled with anger. He stood up and went straight to Bhuqa, who stood up at once and looked at Duma with a steady eye. Duma had felt for his parents in their grief and had not said anything unpleasant against his dead sister. But when he saw Bhuqa, his resolution snapped. His mind went flying back to the day of the court case, the day when he last saw Bhuqa.

'Satanandini!' he shouted, in a voice like the bark of a dog. 'What do you want here? Have you come to rejoice, to sing "The bitch is dead!" As you did on the day of the court case? Are you not content to have made my sister a whore? Have you come now to view the results of your work? This time you will not escape. You have visited her just once too often.'

Mlenzana and one or two other men had jumped to their feet and were standing on either side of Bhuqa, ready to protect him if there was need. Bhuqa did not speak. He looked Duma steadily in the eye. He was not frightened of Duma's threats, but he was shocked at his hatred. It had the same quality as the hatred in his father's eye when he spoke to him of Zuziwe. His father's hate had led to Zuziwe's death. Would Duma's hatred lead to the death of some other person? Would it pass down from generation to generation and stand in the way of two young lovers in the future as his father's hatred had stood in the way of his marriage to Zuziwe? Zuziwe had not been rejected by his father because of her personal faults. She had been a victim of the terrible feud instead of being an example for people of goodwill to follow.

Duma looked round, picked up a stout block of wood and advanced on Bhuqa. Mlenzana and old Dakada held down his arms. The women screamed. The men shouted: 'Hayi, Bhele, hayi!' and pleaded with him.

'This is not a day of anger and violence, Bhele,' said Dakada. 'It's a day of sorrow. You ought to show respect to the dead and sympathy to your wounded parents. Let it be far from you to touch their wound with rough fingers. Treat it with gentle fingers so that it may heal soon.'

'When you have removed this limb of Satan from my home, I will be gentle and respectful,' shouted Duma, trying to free himself. 'How can I stand by and see the devil coming to my home with more evil? If you had concern for my home, you would help me destroy the devil and rid the village of him.'

Some men led Bhuqa away from Duma, who tried to follow. But Mlenzana and Dakada held him back. Duma pushed Mlenzana away from him.

'Kwedini, Mlenzana,' he said, stammering in his great

anger, 'have you forgotten what you are, a thing circumcised only yesterday? How dare you hold me? Who are you to teach me what to do? I'll wipe you off together with that son of Satan if you are not careful.'

'Duma, nyana, calm yourself,' said Vukubi Langa, who had come from the main cottage. Mvangeli had been told of Duma's conduct and had asked Vukubi to go and speak to him.

'Any man who remains calm when he sees the killer of his son is not fit to be called a man,' replied Duma.

'Duma, have you gone mad?' Vukubi asked in an angry voice. 'Call back your senses, man. It is true I lost a son and you have lost a sister. But that is not reason enough for you to desecrate a funeral. How can Zuziwe rest in peace if you fight over her open grave?'

'Please, mkhuluwa,' added Mlenzana, 'please remember that Zuziwe hated violence—'

'Kwedini! Shut your mouth,' shouted Duma.

'No, mkhuluwa,' replied Mlenzana, in a firm, quiet voice, 'I will not shut my mouth. I will speak up and remind you of Zuziwe's hatred of violence. Now that she is dead and her mouth shut for ever, I must be her mouth. Tell me, Bhele, when you have assaulted Bhuqa, when you have crushed him and destroyed him, what will that be worth to you or the people of Kwazidenge? What have the Thembus gained from the death of Katana? What have the Hlubis gained over the years from their victories over the Thembus?'

'It's the tradition of the two villages to fight. You dare not break with tradition. If you did, you would be betraying and provoking the ancestors, for then the blood of those who died fighting would have been spilt in vain. And if you provoke the ancestors, you are doomed.'

'What is it to you,' replied Mlenzana, 'if the Hlubis fought the Thembus in the past? Why do you trouble to remember the evils of the past? What merit is there in an evil tradition? It is not for you to boast about it and uphold it. It is for you to be ashamed of it. Go to the witchdoctors, if you believe in them, and ask them to exorcise the devil of hatred. Go down on your knees, if you are so minded, and ask almighty God to bring nearer the day when we can say the fight has ended.'

'Come, Duma,' said Vukubi, 'the coffin is coming out of the main cottage. Leave your anger behind and come with me.'

The coffin was carried out by six Bhele men and placed in front of the cottage. The mourners gathered round the coffin and the funeral service began. It was a big funeral. Almost every man and woman of Kwazidenge attended it. Some mourners had come from places as far off as Jojo and Mathole. Mvangeli was a popular man. The villagers felt that he deserved a big funeral for his daughter. They came to the funeral to express their sympathy in a concrete way, by their presence. But there was not much evidence of sympathy in their faces, though they seemed to take a keen interest in the funeral proceedings and the grief of the chief mourners. On the surface they wore long faces and dark clothes, but deep down they were in holiday mood, ready to glean as much fun from the funeral as they could. They were ready to go off into suppressed giggles at the slightest provocation.

The customary funeral speeches were made and the

familiar motions of weeping gone through. Bhuqa selected an inconspicuous spot on the outer fringe of the circle of mourners. He stood apparently unmoved, but his heart was bleeding inside him. He was tormented by the inadequacy of the speeches. He felt that the speakers were not doing justice to Zuziwe. Their speeches were negative, apologetic. The speakers seemed to feel she was a guilty woman and their duty was to tread lightly on her guilt. They apparently thought they were being charitable to the dead girl and her family. But it was so absurd, so stupid. Bhuqa felt like rushing forward and shouting loud to all the mourners, to the whole village, telling everybody of the depth of her love, the nobility of her character, the purity of her soul. But he could not do that. There was too much hate in that large assembly of mourners. They would not heed his talk of love and nobility and purity.

When the time came for the people to look at the corpse for the last time as it lay in the coffin, Bhuqa approached and stood staring at the beautiful face. The dead girl looked as if she would open her eyes and light up that sombre presence with one of her sunny smiles. Even in death her face gave a silent message of peace and goodwill and love among men. The young man felt that death had not triumphed over her. She had triumphed over death. That lovely, loving, peaceful face filled his heart with gratitude and inspired his soul with a song of praise for her noble life. Would that her face could continue to shine on all the villagers to the end of time.

Bhuqa left immediately after the burial rites had been completed. He went home to prepare for his return trip to Port Elizabeth. His father spoke to him in the evening about the preparations for his marriage to Nozikade. Bhuqa listened in silence to his father's account of the progress that had been made. The greater part of the lobola had been paid and the negotiations were almost complete. The old man was not upset by Bhuqa's silence. There was nothing to fear now that the Hlubi girl was dead. That death had been a fortunate thing for him and his son. Bhuqa's madness for the girl had been a disease which time would soon cure and Bhuqa would be happily married to a proper Thembu girl. But Bhuqa's heart told him quietly and firmly and persistently that he would never marry Nozikade.

It was indeed strange that Zuziwe's death made Bhuqa feel disinclined to marry Nozikade. He felt that Zuziwe would not rest in peace in her grave if he married Nozikade. He remembered how fiercely jealous of his Thembu girls Zuziwe had been. Bhuqa left his home in mid-afternoon and travelled on horseback to the station which served Kwazidenge, to board the evening train which would take him to Port Elizabeth, arriving at New Brighton station early next morning. Many months passed and Bhuqa did not return. Years passed and Bhuqa did not marry Nozikade. So the cattle which had been paid as lobola had to be counted off as a loss to the Ngoma family. Bhuqa was nearly middle-aged when he finally married in Port Elizabeth a girl of the Bhele clan, whose home had formerly been at Jojo. His father had grown too old to oppose him in his decision and was even glad that his son had at last decided to marry, not a wild, giddy-headed town girl, but a girl with a good, respectable rural background.

About the Author

R. L. PETENI was a writer and professor born in 1915 in the Qoboqobo district, Eastern Cape province, South Africa.

He studied English and Social Anthropology at the University of Fort Hare and taught in schools across Heilbron and Transvaal. He served as president of the Cape African Teachers' Union from 1965 to 1976, during which he returned to the University of Fort Hare to lecture English.

His debut novel, *Hill of Fools* (1976) was the first novel to be published in English by a Xhosa speaker. He later translated the book into Xhosa as *Kwazidenge* (1980) before becoming Chancellor of the University of Transkei in 1989.

Peteni died in 2000.